# THE 3 DETECTIVES
## AND THE
# MISSING SUPERSTAR

# THE 3 DETECTIVES
## AND THE
# MISSING SUPERSTAR
☆ ☆ ☆ SIMON BRETT ☆ ☆ ☆

Charles Scribner's Sons Books for Young Readers
Macmillan Publishing Company
866 Third Avenue, New York, NY 10022
Collier Macmillan Canada, Inc.

Printed in the United States of America
First Edition
10 9 8 7 6 5 4 3 2 1

Library of Congress Cataloging-in-Publication Data
Brett, Simon.
The 3 detectives and the missing superstar.
Summary: The disappearance of Britain's leading
rock star begins an investigation by the Three
Detectives.
[1. Mystery and detective stories]   I. Title.
II. Title: Three detectives and the missing superstar.
PZ7.B7523A125   1986   [Fic]      86-15556
ISBN 0-684-18708-6

**FOR SOPHIE,**
who demanded it

# Contents

# THE 3 DETECTIVES
## AND THE
# MISSING SUPERSTAR

# The Video

Emma Cobbett was bored, even though she knew that all over the world there were girls who would give anything to be where she was at that moment. Reddimixx, with a string of four Number One records behind them, was the most popular group in the country. Their lead singer, Dazzleman, was undoubtedly a superstar. And Emma Cobbett was in the same film studio as Reddimixx and Dazzleman.

It was her father who had arranged it. Douglas Cobbett was a film director, and he was working on the video for Reddimixx's latest single, *No Love Lost*. The four minutes of action were being made with as much attention as a full-length film, and even after expensive shooting in Jamaica and Switzerland there was still a lot to be done in the studio.

In three months' time, just before the disc of *No Love Lost* went on sale, the video would be seen for the first time on television. And that showing would probably

1

send another of the group's records to the top of the charts.

It was for the second-to-last day's filming that Douglas Cobbett had arranged for his daughter and her friend to come into the studio and watch. He had had to ask permission for the visit, from every member of the group and a lot of the studio technicians. But, except for one of Reddimixx's road managers, a tall, bearded man everybody called "Stick," none of them minded, so long as the girls sat quietly and didn't get in anyone's way.

Emma knew that for this occasion she *had* to invite Kimberley Dolan. Kimberley was in her class, and she was such a keen Reddimixx fan that it would have been cruel not to include her. Kimberley thought Dazzleman was the most fantastic creature who had ever walked the earth.

So the day had started in great excitement. Kimberley had stayed overnight at the Cobbetts', and what with giggling and deciding what they were going to wear the next day, the girls hadn't gotten a great deal of sleep. Kimberley had insisted on getting up at six to do her hair, a process that, with her current style, took a long time. Emma contented herself with just running a brush through her own light brown hair, but she couldn't help catching some of Kimberley's excitement.

And when they got to the studio, at eight o'clock the next morning, the excitement didn't go away. There was a little crowd of girls outside the entrance, hoping to get Reddimixx's autographs, and Emma and Kimberley felt very important as they were allowed inside.

Although the group was not yet there, the studio was already buzzing with people. Douglas Cobbett just had time to find the girls a corner in which to sit before he got swept up into discussions about the day's filming.

The main studio setting was the dungeon of a haunted castle. Even seen close, it looked very real to Emma and Kimberley. The stone walls seemed to drip with water, and it was quite a shock when one was moved around to reveal that behind it was only wood and canvas. A man with an aerosol can was spraying cobwebs over the dungeon's broken-down table and chair. Another man arrived, carrying a small box with a wire-mesh front. When he opened it, to Emma and Kimberley's horror, two large rats came out. The man laid a little trail of food for them on one of the ledges of the dungeon, and they scuttered along it, collecting the tidbits. Then they waited patiently while he picked them up and put them back in the box. Their rehearsal was over.

After a time the activity on the film set died down. It seemed as if everyone was waiting for something.

It was a quarter past ten, and Emma could see that her father was beginning to get cross. He started pacing up and down, barking out orders to girls with clipboards, who then went scuttling off toward the dressing-room area. It was clear that Reddimixx was late.

One of the girls with clipboards came scuttling back to the director. Emma heard her say, "They're just being made up. Ten minutes at most."

"They knew the call was to start shooting at ten," said her father angrily.

The girl shrugged.

"O.K. Five minutes, everyone," Douglas Cobbett shouted, and came across to where his daughter and Kimberley were sitting.

Emma could see from the tight lines around his eyes that he was still cross, but he smiled at the girls and asked, "All right?"

They both agreed that everything was fine, thank you.

"Nothing's going to happen for another ten minutes or so. If you want to go to get a Coke or something, now'd be a good time."

"No, thanks. We'll wait," said Emma.

"Ooooooh!" An enormous long sigh came out of Kimberley. She pointed with a trembling finger. "Look, it's Darryl."

"Darryl?" Emma echoed.

"Darryl Frost. The drummer," Kimberley murmured.

Darryl's hair, which stuck up in all directions like a lavatory brush, was fluorescent green. He had a green streak of glittery make-up down the bridge of his nose, and from each ear a cluster of green and yellow feathers hung. He was dressed, to fit in with the dungeon scene, in tattered green rags, and a chain joined rings around each of his wrists. But the careless way he swung the chain around suggested that it wasn't made of real metal. To add a final touch to his appearance, he was holding a can of 7-Up with a straw in it.

4

"I'd better go and have a word with him," said Douglas Cobbett.

Over the next five minutes four more members of Reddimixx appeared. They were also dressed in rags and chains. One had very short hair dyed in black and yellow checks. One had tight braided plaits, ending in silver beads. One wore a kind of golden swimming cap, through holes in which spikes of pink hair poked. The last had a black pigtail, with lengths of gold chain plaited into it.

Kimberley thought they all looked fantastic.

"O.K., so let's get on with it," shouted Douglas Cobbett. Then suddenly he stopped. "Where's Dazzleman?"

Darryl the drummer stopped sucking on his straw. "Ah. Looks like he hasn't showed yet, Douggie."

Emma's father put his hands on the sides of his head in despair. "Sharon," he said to one of the girls with clipboards, "go and see if the car's in the car-park. It's the fluorescent green Rolls-Royce." Then he called out, to the studio, "Has anyone actually seen Dazzleman this morning?"

A lot of heads were shaken.

"Oh, no, this is the limit," Douglas snapped. "He's been late for every call there's been. We're way behind schedule. There's no way we're going to get all the filming done."

"Stay cool," said Darryl. "So we book a few more days in the studio . . . So who cares?"

5

Her father did not reply, but Emma could see he strongly disapproved of Darryl's suggestion.

"Stick," Douglas Cobbett called across to the tall, sad-looking road manager, "have you seen him? Or have any of the other roadies?"

The huge man shook his head slowly. "Not since we finished here last night. Last thing I saw was him getting into the car about eight o'clock."

"Any idea where he might be?"

"Just overslept, I would imagine. Unless . . ."

"Unless what?"

The big man was silent for a moment before replying. The other members of Reddimixx shuffled their feet uncomfortably. "Unless he's gone missing again," said Stick at last.

Another loud *"Oh, no!"* was heard from the director, and he pulled at the hair on the sides of his head.

Emma was aware of Kimberley's voice whispering in her ear. "He's done it before. Often. He just disappears for a few days. Weeks even. Once he vanished for two months. I read about it in *Pop Truths* magazine."

"Oh. Where does he go?" asked Emma, also whispering.

"No one knows. He just goes away . . . and then he comes back. I think that's when he gets his ideas for the songs, you know. He's so talented. You can't expect people as talented as that to bother about things like turning up on time."

Douglas Cobbett was now getting extremely angry.

6

"I've never known anything like it! I'm used to working with professionals. I tell you, if Dazzleman doesn't appear in the next five minutes, I wash my hands of the whole business. You can get someone else to make your video for you!"

"Did someone mention my name?"

At the sound of this new voice, everyone in the studio turned toward the main entrance. And there stood Dazzleman.

# ☆ ☆ ☆ 2 ☆ ☆ ☆

# The Autograph

Dazzleman lived up to his name. His entire costume was studded with fake jewels. That day he was wearing a suit cut like a city businessman's, except that, instead of black and gray, its pin-stripes were of glittering gold and silver. The buttons were clusters of gleaming stones, and more of the same encrusted his shoes. Every finger bore a huge, sparkling ring.

But it wasn't just his costume that dazzled. Dazzleman's head was also a ball of glitter. His hair had been shaved away, and silver make-up covered every inch of skin. Over this were streaks of gold glitter-spray. Onto the forehead and cheeks small diamond-shaped mirrors had been stuck, and large globes of crystal hung from the ears. Through all the make-up a pair of brown eyes gleamed mischievously.

"Oooh," Emma felt Kimberley cooing in her ear. "Doesn't he look *fantastic!*"

Nobody on the film set had spoken since Dazzleman's

entrance, and he continued, "Sorry, am I late? I haven't been keeping you all waiting, have I? Oh, I *am* sorry." It could have sounded rude, but Dazzleman managed to keep a little spark of humor in his voice. He had a great deal of charm and he knew how to use it. His voice was ordinary, a rather flat, slack voice, which sounded strange coming from such a magnificently dressed creature.

"Yes, you are late. And we are all extremely annoyed at having been kept waiting." Douglas Cobbett was trying to sound severe but not succeeding. To Emma he sounded just as he did when he was trying to be cross with her two-year-old stepbrother, Tommy, and failing because Tommy was such a clown and made his father giggle.

"I *really* am sorry, Doug. Just have these terrible problems getting up in the morning. Know what I mean?"

This was delivered in such a mock-serious way that Douglas Cobbett had difficulty in holding back a smile. "Come on then. Now you're here, let's get started."

"Sure, Doug. Just got to get into my costume. You don't want to film me in my ordinary street clothes, do you?" asked Dazzleman.

The idea that this walking Christmas tree was wearing "ordinary street clothes" was so ridiculous that everyone on the set burst out laughing, and Dazzleman took the opportunity of the relaxed atmosphere to hurry off to the dressing room.

9

It was then for the first time that Emma became aware of a stocky figure who had followed Dazzleman into the studio. The man wore a gray uniform with a lot of black buttons up the front and carried a gray peaked cap. His small black eyes seemed to dance with humor.

The man in gray came over to the two girls and sat down in a spare chair.

He grinned, revealing uneven rows of large white teeth. "Come to watch the filming, have you?"

They nodded.

The man looked at Kimberley's sweatshirt, on which was printed the letter "I", a large red heart, and the word "Dazzleman" in silver glitter. "Fan, are you, love?" he asked.

"Oh, yes," sighed Kimberley. "I think he's fantastic."

He gave a little grin, which suggested that perhaps he didn't think Dazzleman was quite as fantastic as Kimberley did.

"Anyway, what're your names, girls? I'm Bill, His Nibs' chauffeur."

"What's 'His Nibs'?" asked Kimberley curiously, wondering what fountain pens had to do with it.

"Dazzleman, love. I'm Dazzleman's chauffeur."

"What's a chauffeur?" asked Kimberley, who wasn't really very bright.

"Driver, love, driver," Bill replied, gently, without making fun of her ignorance.

The girls told him their names, and they were soon chatting away. Kimberley wanted to know a thousand details about Dazzleman—what he was like, what he wore around the house, what his favorite color was, what he cleaned his teeth with . . . and so on and so on. Kimberley collected fan magazines full of just that sort of trivial detail, and to have someone sitting beside her who actually knew all the answers was more than she had ever dared to hope for.

"What about food?" she asked Bill. "I read that his favorite sweets are licorice sticks. Is that true?"

"Blimey." Bill laughed. "Don't know where these writers get their information. I tell you, I've worked for Dave"—he corrected himself—"for Dazzleman for over three years, and I've never seen a single licorice stick pass his lips." He leaned forward to Kimberley. "What he does like, though . . . is fish. Shellfish. Lobster he likes, nice fresh lobster. Doesn't like it when it's been frozen, so the local fishmonger has to keep making deliveries."

"That must be expensive," said Emma.

Bill gave a little smile. "I think he can afford it, love."

"Fish, though," said Kimberley slowly. She sounded a bit disappointed. Perhaps she thought fish was too ordinary for someone like Dazzleman. Perhaps she had been hoping for something more rare and exotic. "Why fish?"

"Well, he likes it," Bill replied. "Anyway, it probably helps him get all his ideas for the songs." He grinned again. "Good for the brain, fish."

"Is it?" asked Kimberley. She was silent for a moment, then went on. "I eat lots of fish, and it doesn't seem to make my brain any different."

Bill chuckled, but neither he nor Emma made any comment.

At that moment, Dazzleman appeared from the dressing room, and nearly an hour late, the filming started.

And that was when Emma started to get bored. She had watched her father working before, but it was always a shock to be reminded just how slow filming was. Each shot took so long to set up. The camera was positioned, the lighting arranged, the performers rehearsed, the sound levels checked, and then filming finally began. The first time it was interesting and exciting, but it was never right the first time. So there had to be a second time. And a third time. And a fourth time. And so on, it seemed to Emma, forever.

Kimberley didn't have the problem of boredom. She thought every moment was wonderful. For her, just being in the same building as Dazzleman was like being bathed in sunlight. It was as if all her dreams had suddenly been made real. And when, fairly early in the day, the tape of the new single, *No Love Lost*, was played over the studio speakers, she could hardly contain herself for excitement.

"Do you realize—we're the first people to hear it, Emma! I mean, nobody else at school will hear it for ages. It's not going to be released for about two months. And we're hearing it now. Isn't it *fantastic!*"

Emma nodded and tried to feel properly appreciative of the honor. But to her the song didn't sound that good. She didn't dislike Reddimixx's music. In fact, she had thought their first two Number One singles, *Love Gone Missing* and *Hearts Won't Be the Only Thing (That'll Get Broken)*, were very good indeed. But *No Love Lost* seemed to sound too like the others. It didn't have the same punch.

"They're playing it through to the studio so that the boys can mime to it," Bill explained. "It's not the final version, only a rough mix."

"What's that mean?" asked Emma.

"Oh, *really!*" said Kimberley with scorn, amazed that anyone could be so uninformed about the pop world. "They do the recording with the various instruments and vocals on different tracks and then all the sounds are mixed and remixed until they get a version the producer and everyone else is happy with." She looked at Bill triumphantly. "I'm right, aren't I?"

"You are indeed. They did all the recording at the studio in Dazzleman's house. Producer specially flown in from America. As usual, no expense spared."

The opening bars of *No Love Lost* again throbbed through the studio. Kimberley closed her eyes with pleasure. "Oooh," she breathed. "It's fantastic!"

Lunch was a welcome break for Emma, and the food was good, but still nothing very interesting happened.

The members of Reddimixx were all sitting at one

table. On his own, on the other side of the canteen, sat the mournful Stick, eating food he had brought with him in plastic boxes. (The roadie was a vegetarian, Bill said.) The chauffeur sat with Reddimixx. He had encouraged the girls to join him, but they felt stupidly shy—even Kimberley was afraid of being that close to her idols.

So the girls sat on their own, talking in whispers. Since most of Kimberley's whispers continued to be about how fantastic Dazzleman was, and how fantastic Reddimixx were, and how fantastic *No Love Lost* was, Emma found that the lunch break did nothing to get rid of her boredom.

At two o'clock everyone went back to the studio for more of the same. It was a sunny day outside, and Emma felt wrong returning to the artificial light of the studio. Back to school in two days, she thought, gloomily. There didn't seem to have been much summer that year.

That afternoon work in the studio had slowed down almost to a standstill. They were trying to film a special effect for the video. Because the setting was a haunted dungeon, all of the group members had to look like ghosts for a bit of the action. Dazzleman, in particular, had to look like a headless ghost. This meant that he had to be filmed with his head hidden, and then have film taken of just his head, mouthing the words of *No Love Lost*. The two bits of film would then be joined together, to achieve the final effect of Dazzleman with his head (singing away) tucked underneath his arm. Emma was

14

prepared to believe that the result would be impressive, but she found the process of getting there *very, very* boring.

After the twelfth attempt to line up the camera in the right position for the shot, she could stand it no longer. She looked at her father, but Douglas Cobbett was so busy that she knew he wouldn't notice whether or not his daughter was in the studio.

She glanced at Kimberley. Her friend's hair was braided into a dozen small plaits; on her cheeks and eyelids glitter-spray glinted. There was an expression of intense concentration on her face. She hardly dared blink, in case she missed something that was going on in the studio.

Emma picked up her bag and leaned across to her friend. "Going to slip outside for a breath of air. You coming?"

Kimberley shook her head wordlessly. Her eyes were still fixed on the gleaming figure of Dazzleman.

Emma walked quietly to the exit to the car-park.

Outside it was as lovely as she had hoped. The weather seemed to be apologizing for having been so dull through July and August. The sky was unbroken blue, and the trees that surrounded the studio car-park were giving a last burst of bright greenness before they changed for autumn.

The path that led from the studio door to the car-park was lined by a low wall, and Emma sat on this with relief, basking in the warmth of the sun. The air tasted clean after the unnatural chill of the air-conditioned studio.

She took her book out of her bag, found her place, and began to read.

The sound of a car approaching made her look up. The car was moving fast, its engine revving fiercely.

She knew instantly whose it was. There are not that many people who own fluorescent green Rolls-Royces.

Dazzleman's car halted in a flurry of gravel at the end of the path, only a few yards away. Then it reversed, so that its back faced her. She did not have time to see the driver's face, but she knew it was not Bill. The head was a different shape. The back-view that she could see through the car's rear window looked odd, and it was a moment before she realized that the driver had one ear missing.

Then she heard the clang of the studio door behind her, and Dazzleman emerged, blinking, into the sunlight. He looked at the car and started walking toward it, slowly, mechanically, as if he were a clockwork toy.

Then he saw her. He hesitated and glanced back toward the studio building. Seeming to make a decision, he came toward her.

"Want an autograph, do you, eh?" he said, taking the book out of her hands.

"Well . . . not particularly," Emma said. Then, realizing that that might sound rude, she went on, "I mean, I wasn't sitting here on purpose so that you . . ."

But Dazzleman did not appear to hear what she said. Producing a gold pen from inside his glittering suit, he flicked the book's pages back and scribbled over the title page.

"There you are, love," he said. As he handed the book back to her, he looked into her eyes. His expression was strange. The gleam of mischief Emma had noticed before was gone. In its place was something different, an expression that looked almost like fear.

"Must go," Dazzleman said abruptly. With a last glance at the studio, he marched down to the Rolls-Royce. As he neared it, the driver reached around and opened the back door. Dazzleman got in and slumped into the seat.

As soon as the door closed, the engine revved again, and the car leaped forward. It shot across the car-park and out onto the main road.

"Oh, no!"

Emma turned to the voice behind her and saw Bill, who had just come out of the studio door. Behind him in the shadows she could see the tall bearded figure of Stick. Both of them were looking after the vanished green Rolls-Royce.

"Oh, no!" Bill repeated. "Dazzleman's gone missing again!"

# ☆ ☆ ☆ 3 ☆ ☆ ☆

# Gone Missing

There was no reason now to stay in the car-park. The afternoon did not seem so peaceful anymore. Emma put her book in her bag and followed Bill back into the studio.

"It's a blooming cheek," the driver was muttering. "Getting someone else to drive the Roller for him. That's my job. If he wanted to go missing again, he could at least have asked me to drive him. Three years I've done everything for him, and this is how he repays me."

Emma interrupted his mutterings. "You mean he's told you the other times he was going to go missing?"

"Well, usually, yes. He's kind of given me a hint, you know. Said he might be off for a bit."

"Do you know where he goes?"

"It varies. Usually abroad. I mean, the sort of money he's got, he can go anywhere in the world at an hour's notice."

18

"But doesn't he get recognized?"

"Course not. Think about it, Emma love. O.K., he's an internationally famous pop star, but how many of his millions of fans know what he really looks like? I mean, how many of them have seen him without the make-up?"

"But surely the shaved head makes him conspicuous?" Bill shrugged. "Not so much these days. Hundreds of kids do peculiar things to their hair. Anyway, Dave—Dazzleman's got a whole range of disguises—wigs, beards, moustaches, glasses, the lot."

"But if he goes abroad, he must need a passport."

"And he's got one. Listen, love, you don't think it says Dazzleman on his passport, do you?"

"No, I suppose not."

"Says his real name, doesn't it? David Smith. Pretty ordinary name. So, O.K., the fans all know that's his name, but if you see a bloke called Dave Smith at an airport and he's got red hair and a moustache, you aren't immediately going to think he's Dazzleman, are you?"

Just then they entered the main studio and were quickly surrounded by members of the film crew.

"Well, where is he? Where's Dazzleman?" asked Douglas Cobbett.

"Who knows?" Bill shrugged. "He's only done another bunk, hasn't he?"

"Oh, no!" said Douglas.

"What, you mean he's gone missing again?" asked Darryl. He looked worried under his make-up.

19

"Exactly that," said Bill. "Got in some new driver and gone off to . . . I don't know . . . to get away from the pressure. Isn't that what he usually says?"

Darryl nodded dumbly. "I don't know. Why does he keep doing it?"

"Publicity," said a deep voice, and they all turned to the tall figure of Stick. "That's why he's done it in the past, isn't it? It's always been a publicity stunt."

"But why *now*?" asked Darryl.

"Well, you've got *No Love Lost* about to come out. Wouldn't hurt to have a few newspaper stories drawing attention to the group, would it?"

"But this is too early. The single isn't released for a couple of months."

"He did a bunk before the second one came out, didn't he? And the third."

"Yes, but nearer the time," Darryl argued. "I mean, say we get a story in the newspapers about him disappearing this week . . . well, everyone's going to have forgotten about it by the time the disc comes out. You weren't around the other times he did it, Stick. Then I'm sure part of the reason was publicity. But then we'd got everything ready. This time we haven't even settled the final mix. The plans for the promotional tour are still all up in the air. And we haven't even finished the video, have we?"

"No, we most certainly haven't," agreed Douglas Cobbett angrily.

"Do you reckon we've got enough there, Douggie?"

20

asked Darryl. "I mean, can you cut something together out of the stuff we done in Jamaica and Switzerland?"

The director shook his head firmly. "No chance. Apart from anything else, we've really only done background stuff. Very few close-ups. And almost nothing of Dazzleman himself. I mean, what is Reddimixx without Dazzleman?"

"What we've got at the moment," said Darryl glumly.

"Maybe he's just nipped off to do some shopping or something," said Douglas Cobbett. But he didn't sound very convinced about the idea. "Look, it's half-past four now. We'll give him an hour. If he's not here by half-past five, we'll call it a day."

Half-past five arrived, but there was no sign of Dazzleman. Grumpily, the film crew disbanded and the members of Reddimixx went off to change out of their rags and chains.

For Douglas Cobbett the day was not yet over. He had to have an emergency meeting with his production staff to see how they were going to deal with this new crisis.

So he called Emma and Kimberley over to him, apologized that he wouldn't be able to drive himself, and arranged for a hired car to take them home. His final words were, "Tell Mummy I'm likely to be very late." He spoke grimly, and the lines around his eyes were very tight.

It was an unusual luxury for the two girls to be driven home in such style, but neither of them felt particularly

21

excited about it. The day's abrupt interruption and the last hour of hanging around had left them both tired and gloomy. Emma was also angry to see how much extra work for her father Dazzleman's behavior had caused.

Kimberley looked sad, too, but Emma reckoned that she was only upset at being separated from her idols.

"Oh, I wish he hadn't gone away like that," Kimberley finally said, with tears in her eyes.

"So do I," Emma agreed with some force.

But Kimberley was away in a dream of her own and did not seem to hear. "To think that I've just spent a whole day so close to him, and now I'm going away and I haven't even got an autograph."

Big tears welled up and threatened to ruin her make-up.

"Well, if that's all that's worrying you," said Emma briskly, "you can stop crying. I've got his autograph."

"And don't you want it?" asked Kimberley.

"No, I don't," Emma replied. "I didn't ask for it, but he insisted on giving it to me. And now, after the way he behaved to Daddy, I certainly don't want it."

"But doesn't it say 'To Emma' or something?"

"I'm sure it doesn't. He didn't ask my name." Emma reached into her bag. "And he had the nerve to write in my book. I hate having my books scribbled over."

She opened the book at the title page. "Thank goodness it was only a paperback. If it had been a hardback, I'd have been really cross." She tore out the page. "There, you're welcome to it."

There was a long silence from Kimberley, and then she said, "I don't understand."

"Don't understand what?" asked Emma, turning wearily to her friend.

"This. What he's written. Look." Kimberley pointed to the torn page.

This is what Emma read:

NO 2 S1 T5—THIS IS FOR REAL—DAZZLEMAN

The writing was neat and clear. There was no danger of their misreading the message.

"What on earth does it mean, Emma?"

"I've no idea," she replied slowly.

But her mind was racing. It was putting details together, linking strange things that had happened during the day. Most of all, it was thinking of the expression in Dazzleman's eyes as he had left her, the expression that had looked like fear.

"I wonder . . ."

"Wonder what, Emma?"

"Oh, nothing, Kimberley. Nothing."

And it was nothing that she could tell Kimberley. Emma kept the rest of the sentence silent in her head. But, if she had finished it, she would have said, "I wonder if this is a case for the Three Detectives . . ."

☆ ☆ ☆ **4** ☆ ☆ ☆

# The Second Detective

Emma did not get a chance to talk to Stewart Hinde until after school on the first day of the new term. He was
in the class below her, and every time they might have
talked during the day, Kimberley was around. Emma did
not want Kimberley to hear what she had to say.

They were going through the school gates when Emma
caught up with Stewart and said, "Want to talk."

He nodded, understanding immediately. "Now?"

"No. Can I come 'round to your house after tea?"

"Fine." He nodded again, then suddenly ran off.
Emma watched him go. Stewie was incapable of looking
tidy. He had outgrown his blazer and had managed to
tear one of the side pockets. His shirt stuck out like a
little skirt at the top of his trousers, and the knot of his
tie was invisible under his collar. His straw-colored hair
wouldn't have recognized a brush if it saw one.

After her tea, Emma avoided her stepbrother,
Tommy, who always wanted to play, and hurried to

Stewie's house. It was rather dilapidated, smaller than the Cobbetts' and with an apologetic air. Mr. Hinde had lost his job the year before, and though he had applied for many others, none had worked out for him. As a result, Mrs. Hinde worked full-time at the check-out of the local supermarket, while her husband spent a lot of time sitting at home, gloomily reading the newspapers.

Stewie answered the door and hurried Emma through the house to the back garden, which was rather overgrown, but which contained the rickety shed where Stewie spent much of his time.

He opened the door and said proudly, "Something I want to show you."

"Another invention?" asked Emma.

Stewie nodded mysteriously and pointed to something in the corner of the shed. It was about four feet high and was covered with an old sheet. If Emma had had to guess from the outline what was underneath, she would have said it was a telescope on a stand.

"What is it?"

But he wouldn't be hurried. Taking a pinch of the sheet between thumb and forefinger, he turned to her solemnly. "Madam," he said in a posh voice, "you are honored to be the first person in the world—apart from its inventor—to see this new miracle of modern technology, an invention that will be of untold benefit to man, woman, and child. Madam, may I present you with . . ." He paused for effect, then, with a flourish, stripped the sheet off. ". . . the Stewart Hinde Mark Three *Gunge-Spludger!*"

What he revealed looked very like a telescope. There was a high stand, supporting a tube, about a yard long. On top of the tube a large funnel was fixed, and at one end there was a handle.

Stewie turned to Emma with a smile. "Not bad, eh?"

"Not bad at all. Mark Three, did you say?"

"Yes."

"What happened to Marks One and Two?"

"Ah, I'm afraid they had to be abandoned in the planning stages. Looked good, but didn't work."

"And this one does?"

"I'll show you."

Stewie reached for a plastic freezer box, took off the lid, and dug into the contents with a trowel. What he pulled out was a gooey gray mess that looked rather like well-chewed chewing-gum. He ladled some into the funnel at the top of his invention. Then he pulled back the handle, and about two feet of a smaller cylinder slid out of the main tube.

Still silent, and with great ceremony, he went across to the shed's window and opened it. He returned to stand behind his invention, steadying the tube with his left hand and holding the handle with his right.

"And now, madam," he announced in his daft posh voice, "allow me to demonstrate. Do you see that apple tree over there?"

It was about ten yards away, through the window.

"Yes, I see it."

"And, madam, do you see that circular stump where a branch has been cut off?"

"Yes."

"Keep watching that stump then, and stand by for action. Five . . . four . . . three . . . two . . . one . . . *Action!*"

As he spoke the word, Stewie suddenly pushed the handle forward. The smaller cylinder slid back into the larger, there was a slurping noise, like the last of the bathwater going down the drain, and from the end of the tube a round gray blob shot forward.

It landed with a satisfying splat on the apple tree exactly where the branch had been cut off. And it stayed there, spread and stuck, like a custard pie on a clown's face.

Stewie turned to Emma and bowed solemnly. "The Stewart Hinde Mark Three Gunge-Spludger," he announced again.

"It's marvelous." Then, with a little giggle, she asked, "But what's it for?"

"Ah." He shook his head slowly. "That is the one thing I haven't worked out yet."

She laughed.

Stewie closed the window. Then he replaced the sheet over his invention, Finally, he turned back to Emma. "You wanted to talk?"

She nodded.

"Is it Three Detectives work?"

"I think it could be."

Very quickly she told him of the events of her day in the studio, of Dazzleman's disappearance, and of his strange note.

"What do you think?" she asked.

"I think," said Stewart Hinde, "that we should go and see Marcus."

# ☆ ☆ ☆ 5 ☆ ☆ ☆

# The Third Detective

Marcus Cone's father was international sales manager for a British electronics company. He earned a lot of money, and the house in which the family lived, on a private estate about a mile from Stewie's house, reflected their wealth. There was a double garage and, in the back garden, a swimming pool and tennis court.

Marcus Cone's mother loved travel, and since her husband's work took him all over the world, she went with him as often as she could. The result was that Marcus spent a great deal of time being looked after by a series of housekeepers.

When Emma and Stewie pressed the large brass door-push by the front door, it was opened by the latest of these. She was a large, blonde, vague lady who spoke with a singsong accent, which Emma reckoned was probably Swedish or Danish.

"Good afternoon," said the housekeeper.

"Good afternoon. We are friends of Marcus. Is he in?"

"Oh yes. He is upstairs. Please come with me."

She led them across the large hall and up the wide staircase. There were a lot of bedroom doors leading off the landing, but she continued up a smaller staircase to the attic level.

They were faced by a door painted red. From the other side of it came the blips of some electronic machine. On the door was a large printed notice:

PRIVATE, it said. ENTER ONLY ON URGENT BUSINESS. AND KNOCK BEFORE ENTERING.

The housekeeper knocked obediently. The electronic blips continued. She knocked again. There was still no reaction. Very carefully she turned the handle of the door and gently pushed it ajar.

"Marcus," she began quietly, "some friends of yours have—"

"Ssh!" Marcus did not look away from the screen of his computer.

The housekeeper did not seem upset by his rudeness. She shrugged, ushered in Emma and Stewie, and closed the door softly behind them.

Marcus's dark head remained resolutely turned away from his friends, and they knew him too well to hope to get anything out of him before he finished his program.

Emma and Stewie looked around Marcus's den to see what his latest craze was. This wasn't his bedroom; he slept downstairs. In one corner of the room stood an electronic keyboard; in another, gleaming hi-fi equipment was stacked. There was also a second television, with a video cassette recorder underneath it.

But none of these amusements appeared to have been touched for some time. The litter of floppy discs, manuals, and print-outs on the floor suggested that the computer now ruled Marcus's leisure time.

A final electronic blip sounded. "Right, I'll save that," Marcus announced with satisfaction, and he pressed a key. The computer whirred for a minute and was silent. He removed the discs from both drives, switched off, and turned to his friends.

"Sorry. Had to finish. Do you want a drink or something?"

"I wouldn't mind," said Emma. "It's still pretty hot."

"Yes," Stewie agreed. "If you've got something up here."

"Coke? Lemonade? Bitter Lemon? 7-Up?"

They both asked for Coke. Marcus pressed an intercom button. "Kirsten, could we have three Cokes up here, please? With ice."

Emma didn't know anyone else like Marcus. He had an unusual mind. Like her, he got bored easily, but if something interested him he was capable of spending long hours getting it right.

He also looked unusual. His eyes were very black, and so was his hair, which he always had cut with a dead straight fringe high across his forehead. His skin was naturally smooth and brown, and he was fat. His fatness, one of those things, like the frequent absences of his parents, which might have upset some people, did not worry him at all. He was Marcus Cone, he liked being Marcus Cone, and he didn't really care what anyone else thought.

Emma didn't want to talk seriously until Kirsten had appeared with the drinks.

"How's school?" she asked, making conversation.

"Haven't gone back yet," said Marcus. "Next week."

Of course. Marcus went to a private school and got longer holidays than they did.

"Quite looking forward to going back, actually," he continued. "We've got this teacher who's really into computers, and I've worked out a couple of programs I want to try out on him."

At that moment the three iced Cokes appeared.

"Right," said Marcus, when Kirsten was safely out of earshot. "Why have you come? Is it Three Detectives business?"

He spoke with enthusiasm. Detective work was one of the subjects that really interested him.

"Yes," Emma replied. "I think it could be."

"What is it? Something been stolen?"

"Perhaps."

"Money? Jewels? Paintings? What?"

"A superstar," said Emma.

She filled him in on the circumstances of Dazzleman's

disappearance. Stewie had listened to her in silence, but Marcus kept interrupting, questioning details, asking for more information. When she had finished, he had another question. "You say that Dazzleman has often done a bunk in the past. What makes you so sure there's something odd about it this time?"

"The timing's the main thing. From all I've heard, he certainly seems to be a moody person, but he's got what Daddy calls 'a shrewd commercial sense.' For Dazzleman to disappear now doesn't make commercial sense. The final mix on the new disc isn't completed, nor's the planning for the promotional tour—they haven't even finished the video."

Marcus nodded and paced up and down his den a few times in silence. Then he asked, "What's the record like?"

"The new one? Hard to say. My feeling is that it's probably not as good as the previous ones. Why do you ask?"

"Not sure. Just interest, perhaps. I don't know much about pop music—classical's really my thing." Marcus took a few more paces in silence. "Any other reasons you think there's something criminal going on?"

Emma told him about the autograph.

"Have you got it?"

She handed the torn title page over to Marcus. He looked at it for a long time.

"Hmm," he said eventually. "And you've no idea what it means?"

"I think it's a code," said Stewie.

Marcus nodded slowly. "I think you could be right. But why would he want to give a message to you, Emma?"

"I don't know. Perhaps because I was the only person around at the time."

"Maybe."

"I sometimes work out codes with friends at school," said Stewie, "but I've thought about this one and I don't see any obvious way of breaking it."

"No. The only way with codes is to try out thousands and thousands of different possibilities until you find one that makes sense."

"That could take forever," complained Emma.

"Yes. Mind you," Marcus tapped the keyboard in front of him, "it's the kind of thing the computer could do in no time."

"Could it?"

"Yes. What would take the time, though, would be working out the right program."

"Do you think you could do it, Marcus?" asked Stewie.

"Given enough time, yes. I'd certainly be prepared to have a go."

"Before you go to those lengths," said Emma, "let's just think if there is something obvious we're missing. It may not even be a code."

"No," Marcus screwed up his face. "I feel a bit lost, not knowing anything about pop music. Before I make a start on the case, I need a crash course on Dazzleman, Reddimixx, and everything that has ever happened to them."

"Yes, that's exactly what you need." Emma smiled. "And I know where you can get it."

# NO 2 S1 T5

They went to see Kimberley on Saturday morning. She lived with her mother in a flat over the Green Parrot, the restaurant that Mrs. Dolan ran. There wasn't a Mr. Dolan. (Well, there was, but he didn't live with them. The couple had divorced when Kimberley was two. Mr. Dolan had gone to work in the Middle East, and his daughter hadn't seen him since.)

Saturday mornings were always busy for the restaurant, so Kimberley was on her own when the Three Detectives came to visit her.

No one could have walked into her bedroom without realizing instantly that Kimberley Dolan was a Reddimixx fan. The walls were covered with posters and photographs cut out of fan magazines. Some were of the whole group, some of the individual members of Reddimixx, but most were of Dazzleman himself. Dazzleman scarves hung around the mirror on Kimberley's dressing-table; a plastic Dazzleman figure stood in front of it. On her bed was a silver cushion with Dazzleman's face on it. On her shelves were piles and piles of fan magazines.

Amid the chaos of make-up, bracelets, and badges on Kimberley's desk was a large scrapbook; beside it were a pair of scissors and a newspaper from which she had been cutting something when the Three Detectives arrived.

Marcus walked straight across and looked at the newspaper article. "Is this about Dazzleman?"

"Yes," said Kimberley. "It's the only report I've been able to find about his disappearance. I really can't understand it. I mean, the papers fill themselves up with what's going on in America and Russia and Africa and all that rubbish, and then when something really important happens, they ignore it."

"Maybe they don't think it *is* important," suggested Emma.

"They're 'round the twist if they don't," Kimberley protested.

"Did they make more of a fuss the other times he disappeared?" asked Stewie.

"Yes, they did." Kimberley reached for her scrapbook and instantly found the articles about the previous occasions. "Look—all the papers had something on the story the first time. And most of them did the second. And what they wrote was more friendly—I mean, it's just plain rude what they've written this time."

Marcus, who was still holding the most recent newspaper article, read it out loud.

"'FADING POP STAR GOES AWOL AGAIN. Dazzleman, the—'"

"What's AWOL mean?" asked Stewie.

"It means," said Kimberley with dignity, "that he's flown away. It's a misprint. They got the letters the wrong way 'round. It should be A OWL. They mean he's gone A OWL—in other words, flown away."

"A OWL?" Emma repeated the expression. Somehow it didn't sound right to her.

"Actually," said Marcus patiently, "AWOL is correct. It's Army slang. The letters stand for Absent Without Leave."

"Oh." Kimberley abruptly changed the subject. "Anyway, they've got a nerve to call him a 'fading' pop star. Who do they think they are?"

"If the new single doesn't get into the Top Ten, he will be a fading pop star," said Emma. "Once groups start to lose popularity, it happens very quickly."

"What else does the paper say?" asked Stewie.

Marcus read the rest of the article. "'Dazzleman, the lead singer of Reddimixx and idol of thousands of teeny-boppers, has gone missing again. The sensitive so-called genius makes a habit of this. Before most of the releases of Reddimixx's chart-topping singles, the silver star has disappeared. Can it be coincidence that the group has another release due in eight weeks? A spokesman for his record company said yesterday, "We have no idea where he's gone this time." A phone call to the superstar's two-million pound mansion in Pegler's End produced this reaction from his road manager, Stick Watson: "Dazzleman's a law unto himself. We never know what he's up to." Both spokesmen sounded a little tired of the superstar's antics. Maybe the public will also soon be weary of his publicity stunts and exhibitionism.'"

"What's exhibishiwhateveritwas?" asked Stewie.

"Showing off," said Marcus.

"Well, I think it's a pretty nasty article," complained Kimberley. "Absolute nonsense, too, suggesting that people are getting tired of him. *And,*" she finished angrily, "I am *not* a teeny-bopper!"

"But it's a bad sign," said Emma, "when the papers start writing about him like that. It's only a step from being *called* a fading pop star to actually *becoming* a fading pop star."

"Pegler's End," said Marcus slowly.

"What about it?" asked Stewie.

"Nothing. Except that it's not far from here."

"Yes. So what?"

"Well, if we decided we wanted to go to see his house, it wouldn't take us long—that's all."

"Ooh, if you're going to his house," cooed Kimberley, "please can I come, too? I'd love to see it, just see the outside, just be where he's been, know that I'm standing on the very spot where Dazzleman himself—"

"Oh, shut up, Kim!" snapped Emma, who had heard rather too much of this sort of thing from her friend over the last week.

Before Kimberley had time to burst into tears or even

39

just look hurt, Marcus spoke. "Listen, Kimberley, I know nothing about Reddimixx, and I want to know everything. Emma tells me you're the world's greatest living expert on the subject."

Kimberley was flattered, and her expression changed to a smile. "Well, yes, I do know quite a lot about them."

"Good. Right, please treat me like an idiot and tell me the basic facts. First, how many singles have they produced?"

"Four. *No Love Lost* will be the fifth. All of the first four went to Number One."

"What were they called?"

Kimberley produced all the answers instantly. If only all her schoolwork had been about Reddimixx, she would have been at the top of the class. (Unfortunately, because none of it was about Reddimixx, she usually was at the bottom.)

"The first single was *Love Gone Missing*. That was at the top for three weeks, also Number One in the States. Then *Hearts Won't Be the Only Thing (That'll Get Broken)*. Top of the charts for five weeks. Then they did *All Gone Sour* and *Padlock on My Heart*. Both stayed at the top for two weeks."

Marcus looked thoughtful. "So maybe they *are* past their peak of popularity."

"No, they're not!" Kimberley snapped. "They're still megastars. Their third album's still at the top of the album charts."

"I see. Who writes the songs?"

"Dazzleman. He's fantastic. He can do anything."

"Yes. Maybe. Have you got any of their records, Kimberley?"

"Have I got any?" She gave a little laugh. "Marcus, I have got all of them. Every single single—and the twelve-inch versions—and the picture-discs, when they've issued those—and all three albums. I have got every sound Reddimixx have ever recorded."

"Well done," said Marcus. "I'd like to hear some of it."

"No problem." Kimberley reached across to her portable cassette-player and a stack of boxed cassettes. "These are the albums. I haven't got my own record-player, so if we want to listen to the singles we'll have to use Mum's in the living-room."

"I wonder," said Marcus. "Do you think I could borrow the albums? Listen to them at home?"

Kimberley looked doubtful. "They're very precious. I do listen to them a lot. If anything happened to them . . ."

"I'd take great care. And bring them back tomorrow. I promise."

"Well . . ."

"It's just that I really do want to have a proper listen to them. If they are as good as you say . . ."

"Of course. They're absolutely brilliant! And not just the singles. I mean, some of the tracks on the albums are amazing! The third track on the first album is out of this

41

world, and then the sixth and the seventh on *Number Two*—that's Side One, they're excellent, really excellent. And the latest album, well, the whole thing is absolutely—"

*"Stop!"*

It was so unlike Stewie to interrupt that they were all silent and looked at him.

A little smile played around the corners of his mouth. "I think," he said slowly, "that I have worked out the code."

*"What?"*

"It was NO 2 S1 T5, wasn't it?"

"Yes."

"Suppose that referred to one of the albums . . ."

"What do you mean?"

"Kimberley, you said the second Reddimixx album was called *Number Two*?"

"That's right."

"Well, N O is a short way of writing 'number.'"

"And S1?" asked Emma.

"Side one."

"And T5 is—"

"Track five!" said Stewie triumphantly.

Emma was very excited. "You mean there'll be a message in the song?"

Stewie nodded. "I think so."

It didn't take a moment for Kimberley to fit the tape into the cassette-player and spool through to the right track. She and the Three Detectives listened in silence as

42

Dazzleman's strange, rasping voice sang.

Through the electronic jangling of the accompaniment, the words were clear. And so was their message.

*"I'm in trouble,*
*All alone.*
*I'm like a prisoner*
*In my own home.*
*Only you can save me*
*From my misery,*
*And if you can find me,*
*You can set me free.*

*I'm so lonely,*
*Locked away.*
*I can't remember*
*The light of day.*
*I'm a long-term prisoner*
*Under lock and key,*
*Who only you can rescue—*
*You can set me free.*

*I'm so helpless*
*Without you.*
*If you don't save me,*
*My life is through.*
*Only you can give me*
*Back my liberty.*
*If you find my prison,*
*You can set me free.*
*Yes, if you find my prison,*
*You . . . can . . . set . . . me . . . FREE!!!"*

They remained silent after the song ended. Then Kimberley, who had been bobbing her head and tapping her toes throughout, said, "Great track, isn't it?"

The others nodded.

"But I don't think it means anything in particular, do you?"

"Oh, yes, it does," said Stewie.

"Then what?"

"It means, Kim," said Emma, "that Dazzleman has been kidnapped."

## ☆ ☆ ☆ 7 ☆ ☆ ☆

# Trouble for Douglas Cobbett

On Monday morning at breakfast Douglas Cobbett was in a bad mood.

Breakfast was never the best time in the Cobbett household. Emma's stepmother was, as she kept saying, "bad in the mornings," and the result was that breakfast could be noisy. There was a lot of shouting at people to get up, brush their hair, do their piano practice, and so on. Emma loved her stepmother dearly (her own mother had died when she was a baby), but she found it was a good idea to keep out of her way in the mornings, or she'd become involved in all the shouting.

Anyway, she felt her stepmother had quite enough on her hands with two-year-old Tommy making patterns of jam and milk on the kitchen table. So Emma always tried to eat her breakfast quickly and get out of the house as soon as possible. She knew that by the time she

45

got home from school her stepmother would be fully awake and generally much nicer to be with.

Monday's was always the worst breakfast of the week, and this particular Monday breakfast was made even worse by her father's mood.

The Cobbett household was very influenced by what came in the post. A sudden unexpected check through the letterbox in the morning could brighten up the whole family for the day. Then Douglas would feel rich and decide that they all deserved a treat, something for the house, a new game for the children, even—if it was a very big check—a holiday.

But the morning post was just as likely to bring bad news—rejection of one of Douglas's ideas for a television program, a letter from one of his favorite actors saying that unfortunately he couldn't take part in the new play Douglas was directing, or—worst of all—a tax bill.

It was clear to Emma from the expression on her father's face that Monday morning that the post had contained bad news.

At least Douglas Cobbett didn't keep things to himself. When he had bad news, he told the whole family what had happened.

"Oh, no!" he wailed as he read the letter.

Emma's, Mrs. Cobbett's, and even Tommy's eyes immediately turned to him. "What's up?" asked his wife.

"It's no great surprise, but it's still infuriating," said Douglas. "This is from the production company making the Reddimixx video. I'm no longer working on it."

"You mean you've been *sacked*?" asked Emma, appalled.

"Not exactly, love. But I might as well have been. This has been building up ever since Dazzleman disappeared. The production company wants that video completed."

"But so do you."

"Of course I do, Emma, but I want it completed *the right way*. They want me just to cut together the film we already have, knock together something out of it."

"Is it possible?"

"It's possible, yes, but that's not the way I work. I could cut something together as they ask, but it wouldn't be my sort of film—it wouldn't be something I'd be proud of."

"So what happens if you refuse to do as they ask?"

Douglas Cobbett shrugged. "I'm taken off the project, and they bring in some director who doesn't care about it, and he cuts the film into something that won't be very good, but that'll just about do."

"Can they do that to you?"

"Oh, yes."

"And then don't you get paid?"

"I get paid off. Get part of the money I should get. But it's not the money that's important."

"It's not *un*important," said Mrs. Cobbett, who knew the problems of running the household when there was no money coming in.

"Don't worry, love." Douglas Cobbett gave his wife a

47

sad grin. "I'll get some other work. In fact, there was something else I was offered last week. My agent said I couldn't do it, because I was tied up on the Reddimixx thing, but now I'm no longer tied up on the Reddimixx thing, I suppose I'll have to."

"Was it something exciting you were offered?" asked Emma.

Her father let out a short laugh. "Hardly. An extremely dull job at the BBC. They're doing yet another of those 'Where are they now?' programs . . . you know, where they search out people who used to be famous a few years ago and find out what they're up to now. The director's been taken ill, and they need someone to step in and take over for a few weeks. It's not a difficult job, but it would be *very, very* boring." He sighed. "Still, I suppose I'll have to do it. Unless, I suppose, Dazzleman suddenly appears from wherever he's gone to, ready to complete the filming."

Emma suddenly saw a new, important reason to find the missing superstar. "You don't suppose," she began, daring to mention her suspicions, "that Dazzleman might have been kidnapped?"

Douglas Cobbett laughed. "Sorry, love. I think you've been reading too many detective stories. No, he's done it before and I'm sure he'll do it again. I've tried to find out where he is. I've rung practically everyone who knows him. I've been over to Pegler's Hall and asked his staff. No one has a clue. Mind you, I'm pretty certain he's sunning himself on some beach somewhere —Florida, Mexico, the Seychelles, who can say?"

"Well," said Emma, jutting out her chin with determination, "I'm going to find out where he is, and I'm going to get him back into the studio and see that he finishes that video as it should be finished."

Douglas Cobbett leaned across and ruffled his daughter's hair. "Thank you, love. I'll leave it to you then."

But he didn't sound as if he believed her.

Then Tommy knocked over his cup. Milk flooded across the table. At the same moment Mrs. Cobbett looked at her watch.

"Oh, no!" she cried. "Emma, you should have left for school!"

## ✩ ✩ ✩ **8** ✩ ✩ ✩

# Pegler's Hall

"The interesting thing about Reddimixx's music," said Marcus, as the Three Detectives traveled by bus to Pegler's End after school on Tuesday, "is that it gets worse."

"What do you mean?" asked Stewie.

"Well, I listened to those tapes Kimberley lent me. It's not my usual kind of music, but I was very impressed by the early songs. They've got strong melodies, clever tunes that really stay with you. I'm not surprised the group was so successful. Before I heard the music, I thought they'd got to the top because of all the publicity and the ridiculous costumes and the make-up. But no, they really are good."

"Kimberley would be delighted to hear you say that," Emma observed with a grin.

"Yes, but what's strange about it," Marcus continued, "is how suddenly the music stops being good."

"When?" asked Stewie.

"After the third single. *Love Gone Missing,* the first one, is absolutely brilliant, the sort of song that's going to become a standard. That'll be around forever, lots of other groups'll play it and put it on their albums. The second one, *Hearts Won't Be the Only Thing (That'll Get Broken),* well, that's nearly as good. Then *All Gone Sour,* the third one, again is a terrific tune—really strong. But after that, something happens."

"What?"

"It's hard to explain. It's a musical thing. I suppose I could break it down technically and show the difference, but it's more a feeling in the music. The tunes just aren't as rich. They aren't as original. They sound too like the others."

"That's what I noticed in what I heard of the new one, *No Love Lost,*" said Emma.

"I'm sure it'll still sell," said Stewie.

"Oh, yes, it's bound to," Marcus agreed. "The group's built up such a following that they could sell readings from the telephone directory. But it won't go on forever. After a time, unless the standard of the actual music keeps up, the public is going to lose interest."

"And, like the paper said, Dazzleman will be a fading star."

"That's right, Emma. But it is odd—the suddenness with which the quality changes."

"Maybe it's different people writing the songs," suggested Stewie.

Marcus nodded. "That was my first thought. So I

51

looked at the details on the cassette boxes. And, according to those, every single song the group has recorded was written by D. Smith—in other words, by Dazzleman himself."

"Maybe he's just running out of ideas?" said Emma.

"Yes, that's the only explanation that I could think of," Marcus agreed. "The early songs show that he's got an enormous talent as a composer, but maybe he's run out of good ideas and now all he can do is repeat himself."

"Lots of pop groups do that," observed Stewie. "Every record they bring out sounds exactly like the last one."

Emma nodded. "Yes, but most of those groups aren't very original, anyway. They don't have the kind of songwriting talent Dazzleman has in the first place."

"Right," said Marcus. "But for someone who is as good as that, it must be pretty unpleasant. I mean, he must know that his songs are getting worse and worse."

"Yes, he must."

"So I was just wondering whether his running out of ideas had anything to do with Dazzleman's disappearance."

But Marcus didn't get a chance to explain what he meant. The bus slowed to a standstill, and the conductor shouted, "Pegler's End!"

It wasn't difficult to find Dazzleman's house. Pegler's End was a small village, and there was only one property in it big enough to be a superstar's mansion.

The grounds of Pegler's Hall were surrounded by a flint wall, about ten feet high, which seemed to run for miles. The house was set in many acres of land. The Three Detectives could see the tops of trees showing over the wall, but nothing else. They followed the wall along toward the main gates.

"What are we actually looking for?" asked Stewie.

"I'm not sure," Emma replied. "I just want to see the place. I've a feeling it may give us some ideas."

Marcus agreed. "In any investigation it's important to get as much background as possible. The more you can understand the people you're investigating— the more you can sort of get inside their skins—the easier it becomes to work out how they're likely to behave."

Stewie wrinkled his nose. "I'm not sure that I'd like to get inside Dazzleman's skin."

"Why not?"

"Don't fancy all that make-up."

The other two laughed.

The main entrance to Pegler's Hall was very impressive. On each side the flint wall finished in little turrets, and between them were high white-painted metal gates, securely locked in the middle. The gates were solid up to about four feet, but above they were made of vertical and horizontal bars like a portcullis. Looking through these, the Three Detectives could see the house itself.

It was set back, at the end of a long gravel drive lined

with thick hedges. An enormous mansion in dull red brick, with lots of roofs at different levels, from which clusters of tall chimneys rose.

"The original building was started in the reign of Queen Elizabeth the First," said Marcus, who was always full of unexpected bits of knowledge. "Mind you, it's been added to a lot since. And modernized."

The house certainly looked as if no money had been spared on it. All the paintwork gleamed. Everything, including the out-buildings and garden, looked almost unnaturally tidy, like something out of a television commercial.

Stewie suddenly pointed to the massive garage at the side of the house. "Look!"

"Good gracious!" said Emma.

The wide up-and-over door was open, revealing the distinctive radiator grille of a Rolls-Royce. The car was fluorescent green.

Stewie did a little jump of excitement. "Do you think that's it? Do you think he came straight back here from the studio? Do you think Dazzleman's just hiding in his own house?"

Marcus soon put a stop to such ideas. "No. He probably did come back here and then went away again. I mean, if he has just gone off on a holiday, he might have come back here for a disguise, then got his driver to take him to the airport. He wouldn't leave the car anywhere else—it'd just draw attention to where he'd gone."

"I suppose so." Stewie sounded disappointed.

"I wonder who his driver was. . . ," said Emma thoughtfully.

"What do you mean?"

"The one who drove him off from the studio. It wasn't Bill, his usual one."

"Did you get a good look at him?"

"Not from the front, no. All I could see was that he only had one ear."

"That should make him easy to recognize if you ever see him again."

"Yes. I wonder if he was the person behind the kidnapping."

"I shouldn't think so." Once again Marcus squashed the idea. "From what you say, the driver didn't get out of the car. Dazzleman appeared to climb into it voluntarily."

"Yes." Emma had to agree.

Stewie was impatient. "Look, now we're here, what are we going to do?"

"There must be someone around," said Emma. "Daddy talked about the 'staff' at the house. We must try and talk to them."

"How?"

"Well, what would be a good reason for someone to come here?"

Stewie shook his head. "Don't know."

"I've got it!" Emma snapped her fingers. "To get an autograph! Stewie, you do it. You ring that bell on the gatepost, and when someone comes, ask them if you can get Dazzleman's autograph."

"All right. But what are you two going to do?"

"We'll keep out of sight."

"And what do I do after I've asked for the autograph and whoever comes says Dazzleman's not around?"

"Try and get talking to them."

"Try and get talking to them," Stewie mimicked. "You make it sound so easy."

"Go on."

"All right. I'll try."

Emma and Marcus moved along the wall, until they were out of sight of anyone on the far side of the gates, and watched Stewie.

He did what he was told. Firmly, he pressed the button on the gatepost, and waited.

He didn't have long to wait. A deep voice, which was somehow familiar to Emma, barked out, "What do you want?"

"Oh, please, sir," said Stewie politely. "I'm a great fan of Dazzleman. I wonder if it would be possible to get his autograph?"

"Forget it," said the voice rudely. "Dazzleman's not here!"

Stewie continued to be very polite. "Do you by any chance know where he is? Or when he'll be back? You see, I'm very keen to—"

"*Scram!!!*" roared the voice.

And it was said with such unpleasant force that Stewie scrammed.

"What did he look like?" asked Emma urgently, as a breathless Stewie rushed up to her.

"Very tall. Beard. Gloomy-looking."

"I thought so. Stick. Dazzleman's road manager."

"I'm sorry. I didn't have a chance to 'get talking to him,'" Stewie apologized.

"No. So we heard. He didn't sound as if he was in the best of tempers."

"You can say that again!" Stewie sighed, and kicked at a stone. "Well, we've tried a direct approach, and we haven't gotten anywhere with that. What do we do now?"

"I suppose we go home," said Marcus glumly.

Emma nodded, and the little group, disappointed, began to walk back along the wall of Pegler's Hall, toward the bus stop.

"One thing was funny," said Stewie, after a few moments. "Funny peculiar, I mean, not funny ha-ha. It was how quickly that bloke Stick appeared. I mean, he must have come from the house, but he didn't have time to hear me ringing the bell and come all that way. It was as if he was expecting me."

"I think he was," said Marcus.

"What do you mean?"

"I wondered what they were when we were standing in front of the gates."

"What?"

"Didn't you notice two sort of boxes fixed on the trees nearest the gates?"

57

"Yes," replied Emma. "I thought they were lights."

Marcus shook his head. "Video-cameras. Part of the security system. A house like that is bound to be well protected against intruders."

"You mean the video-cameras show anyone who tries to get in?"

"Exactly. They are focused on the gates and they relay the picture back to the house. There are probably more on the other entrances. I don't think anyone who shouldn't, ever gets into Pegler's Hall."

"Hmm." Emma looked back wistfully. "I wish we could get inside, though. For some reason, I'm absolutely certain that the key to Dazzleman's disappearance is in there somewhere. I think . . ."

She stopped and looked again. A van had drawn up facing the gates. On its side in blue letters were the words, J. SPINK & SONS. Below that there was some other writing, but it was too far away for them to read it.

As they watched, the gates must have opened, because the van disappeared inside the walls of Pegler's Hall.

"I wonder what that was," said Marcus.

"Deliveries of something, I suppose. Presumably, even with Dazzleman away, the staff has to go on eating."

Emma was about to turn back when she saw more activity by the gate. A man had walked out and was hurrying away in the opposite direction. She could not see his face, but she would have recognized that stocky back-view anywhere.

"Quick!" She grabbed the others by their arms. "We must catch up with him. He may be able to help us."

"Why? Who is he?"

"That's Bill," said Emma. "Dazzleman's chauffeur."

☆ ☆ ☆ **9** ☆ ☆ ☆

# The Big E

The chauffeur was about to get into his own car, an old but highly polished Mini, as the Three Detectives rushed up to him. He turned as Emma called his name.

He didn't look very happy but managed a smile for her. "Hello, love. Emma, isn't it? Fancy meeting you here."

She introduced Marcus and Stewie to him, and the chauffeur shook their hands gravely. "Why are you here, though?" he asked. "Do you live 'round these parts?"

"A few miles away."

Bill still looked curious, as if Emma's reply had not fully answered his question, and she decided that she was going to trust him.

"We're really here," she said, "because this is Dazzleman's house."

"Don't I know it!" Bill shook his head gloomily. "But why are you here? Your mate Kimberley was the big Dazzleman fan. I got the impression that you weren't that interested."

60

"You're right. I'm not that interested in him as a pop star. But I am interested in his disappearance."

Bill looked up sharply at the last word. "What do you mean?"

"Look, you were there when it happened. So was I. And the more I've thought about it since, the more I've thought there was something strange about the way he went off."

"How do you mean—strange?"

"Well, as if he wasn't doing it because he wanted to. As if someone was making him do it. As if he had been sort of . . . kidnapped."

The chauffeur rubbed his chin thoughtfully. "I'm not sure about that. Mind you, there is something odd about the whole business. He's always been moody, always changed his mind a lot, but this time it feels different."

"That's what we think," said Emma "We're determined to get to the bottom of it, and we'd be really grateful for your help—I mean, with you knowing so much about Dazzleman and everything. Please, will you help us?"

There was a silence, then the chauffeur made up his mind. "Yes, of course I'll help you." He looked at his watch. "Tell you what, I feel in serious need of a drink. There's a nice pub a couple of miles along the road. Let's go and talk there."

"But I'm not allowed in a pub," Stewie objected sadly. "Not till I'm fourteen."

"Don't worry, son. The Black Horse has got a garden.

61

You're allowed to sit there." He opened the Mini's doors. "Come on, hop in!"

The garden of the Black Horse was pretty and peaceful. They sat at a wooden table under a tree, sipping the iced Cokes and munching the salt and vinegar crisps that Bill had bought them. He had a pint of bitter. As soon as he had sat down, he took a long swallow that emptied the glass by about a third.

"I needed that," he said as he licked his lips. "Funny sort of day it's been." He looked across at the Three Detectives, sitting in a row on the bench opposite him. "Now, have you got any other reasons to be suspicious about Dazzleman's disappearance?"

Emma, with help from Marcus and Stewie, brought him up to date with their thinking on the subject. She told him about the mysterious autograph and the way they had been able to relate it to the song on the *Number Two* album.

"Phew!" Bill shook his head. "That sounds pretty far-fetched to me."

"But what else could that message have meant? Come on, you must have seen him write thousands of autographs—did you ever see him put anything like that?"

The chauffeur had to admit that no, he never had.

"We think it was a cry for help," said Marcus. "He knew he was going to be kidnapped, he didn't want the driver to realize that he was getting a message out, so he did something that looked perfectly ordinary—signed an autograph for a girl who was waiting outside the studio. But Emma says he looked very strange as he did it."

"He certainly did. I'm sure he was afraid of something."

Bill scratched his balding head. "But what was he afraid of?"

"That's what we've got to find out."

"Bill," Marcus began in a businesslike manner, "what sort of mood was Dazzleman in that morning? You know, the day he disappeared. Did he seem worried about anything?"

"Hard to say, really. Not particularly worried, I don't think. I remember, I got there at eight to drive him to the studio and—"

"Sorry to interrupt," Stewie interrupted, "but you don't live in Pegler's Hall?"

"No. There's a bedroom there that I use quite often . . . you know, if we've got back late from somewhere or he wants me on call for something, but I've my own home here in the village. Blackthorn Cottage, it's called."

"I see. Thanks. Do go on."

"Right. So that morning I get there at eight, to get him to the studio at nine so that he's all made up and in costume for the ten o'clock call. Well, when I get there, he's still asleep."

"Did he sleep in all that silver make-up?" asked Stewie curiously.

"No, he didn't. Put it all on every morning—or at

least every morning when he was working as Dazzleman. Took best part of an hour. So when I found he was still asleep, I knew he was going to be late."

"But, going back to Dazzleman's mood," Marcus insisted, "did he seem particularly nervous or jumpy on the day he vanished?"

Bill shook his head. "Not particularly, no. I mean, his moods have been worse the last six months, but that day wasn't a specially bad one."

"Why do you reckon he's been worse the last six months?" asked Emma.

The chauffeur shrugged. "I don't know. I suppose he was feeling worried about losing touch, losing the success. The last two singles didn't sell as well as the first three. To my mind, they wasn't such good songs."

Marcus nodded, pleased to have his musical opinion confirmed. "In what ways were Dazzleman's moods worse?"

"He was just, like, nervous, ill at ease. Jumpy 'round the house, couldn't really concentrate on anything— know what I mean?"

The Three Detectives nodded.

"And certainly," Bill went on, "up until six months ago, there's no way he'd have treated me like he has."

"What do you mean?"

"He's only given me the Big E, hasn't he?"

Stewie looked blank, as did the others, so he was speaking for all the detectives when he asked, "The Big E—what on earth does that mean?"

"Well, the Big E, it's like the old heave-ho, the push, the shove, the boot . . . You with me yet?"

Stewie shook his head.

"Do you mean," asked Emma, "that you've lost your job? That you've been sacked?"

"That, darling, is exactly what I mean."

Stewie was still curious. "Why did you call it the Big E?"

"Just an expression, son. E for elbow. You give someone the elbow, you push them out—get it?"

Stewie nodded.

Emma was puzzled. "But Dazzleman's disappeared. How could he have given you the sack?"

Grimly, Bill reached into the inside pocket of his jacket and produced an envelope. He handed it over to the Three Detectives and nodded to indicate that they could read the contents.

The writing was the same as the mysterious autograph in Emma's book.

*Dear Bill,* it began, *Thank you very much for all your help to me over the last few years. I am sorry to say that a change in my plans for the future means that I will no longer require your services. I will of course be happy to write you a reference for any future employer, and hope you will accept the enclosed five hundred pounds in lieu of notice. Yours, Dave Smith.*

Stewie pointed to the one word he didn't recognize. "What's 'lie-you'?" he asked, having a go at the pronunciation of "lieu."

"That's pronounced 'loo,'" said Bill.

"Loo?" Stewie echoed. "What, you mean he gave you the five hundred pounds in the loo?"

"No, no." Bill grinned. "'In lieu' is just a posh way of saying 'instead of.'"

"Oh." Stewie looked disappointed. Then he peered inside the envelope. "Where's the five hundred pounds?" To him it seemed an enormous amount of money.

"I wasn't going to take that!" Bill replied angrily. "It was an insult. Three years of loyal service, then he gives me a letter like that and thinks five hundred quid's going to make me feel better about it. Huh—he can keep his five hundred quid!"

"Are you positive it's Dazzleman's writing?" asked Marcus.

"Yes. No question about it. He wrote that."

Emma looked at the date. September 2. "And it was written the day *before* he disappeared."

"Yes, that's what makes me even angrier about it! That day I go and wake him up, hang around till he's ready, drive him to the studio, have lunch with him . . . All the time he's chattering away, very matey . . . and he's already decided he's going to give me the elbow!"

"It suggests," said Marcus, piecing together what had happened, "that he had planned his disappearance in advance."

"Unless the date on the letter's wrong," Stewie suggested. "You can put any date you like on a letter. I mean, unless you actually got it on the day it was written . . ."

"Which I didn't. I just got it this afternoon."

"Through the post?" asked Emma.

"No. By hand. You see, what's been happening is, since Dave did his bunk, I've been staying at home in the cottage. Every morning I've rung in to Pegler's Hall, asked if he's come back, asked if I'll be needed during the day. Each day I've got the same reply—No thanks, you won't be needed."

"Who's answered the phone?"

"Stick. Always Stick."

"So what happened today?"

"Well, I got to thinking—this is daft. Somebody at the house must know something about what's going on, so I thought I'd come up and have a chat with a few people. I've got a key to the gate, so I just walk in, and I meet Stick. And he tells me, straight out, that all the staff's been sacked—"

"All the staff?"

"Yeah—and he gives me the letter and tells me to clear off."

"But he hasn't been sacked?"

"No. He's been put in charge. He shows me this letter Dave's written, which gives Stick complete control over everything during our lord and blooming master's absence."

"And that was in Dazzleman's writing, too?"

67

"Oh, yes. There was nothing funny about it—except what it said."

"So what did you do?"

"Not a lot I could do, was there? I looked at me letter, gave Stick the money, saying I didn't want anything to do with it, and I left. Which was when you saw me coming out the gate."

"And have you still got your keys?" asked Stewie eagerly.

The chauffeur shook his head. "No such luck. Stick said Dave had insisted all keys had to be returned."

"And did he say when Dazzleman had given these orders?"

"According to him, he got back to the house after that day in the studio and found this pile of letters on his desk—Stick has an office in the house, you see. And he says the last time he saw Dave was when he walked out of the studio on the afternoon of September third."

"Which was the last time anyone saw him," observed Marcus.

"Except for me."

"Oh, yes, of course, Emma. But you only saw him a few minutes after. And then he just vanished into thin air."

They were silent. Bill drained the last of his pint and was about to stand up when Emma stopped him.

"Have you any idea what might be going on?"

The chauffeur shook his head. "Only thing I can think is that Dave's ill . . . You know, that he's had some kind of breakdown, something wrong with his mind. Like I say, he's always been a moody sort of bloke, sometimes difficult, sometimes annoying, but what he's done now is right out of character. I reckon he must be ill, and maybe he's gone off somewhere to recover."

"Maybe," Emma suggested encouragingly, "when he has recovered, he'll come back and everything'll be all right again. You'll get your job back."

"Maybe." But Bill's short, dry laugh didn't suggest he thought it was very likely.

Douglas Cobbett wasn't the only one who was suffering from Dazzleman's disappearance. Bill had lost his job. So had all the other members of the staff at Pegler's Hall. Dazzleman had to be found; only he could explain what had been going on.

"Don't worry," Emma said decisively to Bill. "We are going to find him."

# ☆ ☆ ☆ 10 ☆ ☆ ☆

# Where Are They Now?

It was difficult for the Three Detectives to maintain their confidence in the next few days. All the excitement of going to Dazzleman's house and talking to Bill trickled away, and gloom descended.

There were many reasons for thinking that the superstar's disappearance was suspicious, and yet they couldn't link the facts together, couldn't see a pattern in them. Nor could they work out what their next step should be. After the visit to Pegler's Hall, they seemed to be up against a brick wall.

The situation was made worse for Emma by seeing how unhappy her father was. He had been really enjoying making the Reddimixx video, and had hoped that, when it came out, it might lead to more work of a similar kind. But now, instead, he was back for a few weeks at the BBC, working on the kind of program he had done ten years previously. It made him feel as if his career wasn't progressing at all.

And, to make things worse, he knew that some other director was being paid to chop up the film he had already shot of Reddimixx and was turning it into a very ordinary video.

So breakfasts in the Cobbett household were even grimmer than usual, as Emma's father sat, stony-faced, behind his newspaper, only speaking to shout at Tommy when more jam got spilled.

"Is working for the BBC really that awful?" asked Emma one particularly difficult morning.

Her father smiled. "No, love. It's just that I'd got lots of ideas going for that video, and it's terribly frustrating to be interrupted just when it was going so well." He took his daughter's hand. "I've never been very good at pretending everything's wonderful when I don't think it is. Don't worry, though. It's just a matter of time. Soon I'll get used to the idea that the Reddimixx thing is really over. And the program I'm working on isn't that bad. At least, it wouldn't be that bad if only I could concentrate on it. I still seem so full of thoughts for the video that I can't seem to come up with any other ideas."

"What sort of ideas do you need?"

"Well, I told you it's a sort of 'Where are they now?' show. Finding out what people who used to be famous do now. Talking to their friends, that sort of thing. The trouble is, I've got these two very bright researchers just panting to track down these people and see if they'll agree to be on the program—and I can't think of any good names for them to follow up."

"If I think of any, I'll tell you straight away," said Emma.

"Thank you, love." But further conversation was interrupted by Tommy upturning the sugar bowl over his head. The Cobbetts' kitchen became extremely noisy.

"I'm sure it's something in his past," said Marcus. "Usually when people do peculiar things, there's a reason for it in something that happened a long time ago. I just feel that we need to know more about what Dazzleman was like before he became Dazzleman."

"But who can we find out from?" asked Stewie. "We asked Bill most things we could think of, but he couldn't come up with a lot that was very helpful."

"No, but then Bill has only known him for about three years. I want to know what David Smith was up to before that. I want to do a bit of research on him."

"That sounds boring," said Emma crossly. They were all sitting in Marcus's den one day after school. She went across to sit at the electronic keyboard and played a random sequence of notes.

After a moment Marcus stopped her. "I'm sorry. It really is hurting my ears."

"See if I care," Emma snapped. But she did switch off the machine.

"Why are you in such a ratty mood?"

"I don't know." She sighed. "Well, yes, I do know actually. I want to get on with this case, and we don't seem able to. I want to do something positive, take some action—not just sit around doing research."

"We all feel the same," said Marcus patiently. "But what action can we take? What do you suggest we do, Emma?"

"I'm sure we could find the key to this in Pegler's Hall. I think we should have another go at getting inside Dazzleman's house."

"Yes!" said Stewie. "Let's do it!"

Marcus remained annoyingly calm. "Maybe we will have to do that at some point, but we mustn't rush it. If we get caught, we'll be handed over to the police as trespassers. Any attempt to get into that place must be planned to the last detail."

"Hmmph!" Emma grunted. She seemed to spend her life being slowed down by people who wanted to "plan everything to the last detail."

"And, in the meantime," Marcus continued, as calm as ever, "there are other useful things we can do."

"Like?"

"Like, as I said, more research."

"And how are we going to do that?" Emma asked grumpily.

"I think we should pay another visit to your friend Kimberley."

Marcus's hunch had been right. Among the piles of fan magazines in Kimberley's bedroom there were plenty of articles about the members of Reddimixx before they formed the group. He distributed magazines to the other two, and they settled down to read.

Kimberley sat on her bed and agreed to be quiet.

Whenever any of them found anything they thought might be important, they would read it to the others.

The silence lasted less than a minute, and it was Kimberley who broke it. Talking was a disease with her, and she had real difficulty in keeping her mouth shut.

"I think it's rotten, him still being missing," she said. "I mean, what do we have policemen for? They just go around directing traffic and trying to catch burglars and stopping people who are driving too fast, and when something *really serious* happens, they don't do anything."

"I don't think they'd regard it as 'really serious.'"

"Why not? If he's been kidnapped, Marcus . . ."

"We don't *know* he's been kidnapped. We just *think* he may have been."

"Well, I think we should tell the police about our suspicions. Don't you, Emma?"

"I would, Kim, if I thought they'd believe me. I'm sure, if the police have thought at all about Dazzleman's disappearance, they'd think it's just another publicity stunt. And they'd think we were silly little fans making a drama out of it."

"I'm not a silly little fan," complained Kimberley.

"I didn't say you were. I just said that's what they'd *think*."

"We are actually meant to be reading." Marcus spoke like a schoolmaster and they were all silent.

This time Kimberley lasted just over a minute (which was probably some kind of record for her). Then she said, "I know everything about Reddimixx by heart. I've read all those magazines lots of times. So, if there's anything you want to know, why don't you just ask me?"

Marcus had looked up sharply, as if to tell her to be quiet, but he appeared to change his mind. "Yes, you could save us some time. Look, it's obvious from what we're reading that most of Reddimixx had played with a lot of other groups before they formed the band."

"Yes, that's right." Kimberley glowed at the chance to show off her knowledge. "Darryl Frost was with Kukumber Kool, and then with Broken Zips, where he met up with Wayne, who'd come from the Executioners. And then Phil started out with a Manchester group called Holes in Your Sox, but then he split from them and joined a lot from Cardiff called—"

"Yes, yes, yes, fine." Marcus raised a hand to stop this deluge of information. "It's really Dazzleman himself we're interested in."

Kimberley took a breath. "Ah. There's really not so much known about him."

"You mean he just suddenly burst on the scene as Dazzleman? He'd never played with any other bands before?"

"No, he *had* played with other bands, but none of the magazines seem to be able to give a list of them. So far as I can work out, he kept changing his name and his appearance, so nobody knew who he was."

"That would fit, wouldn't it, with what he's doing now. All this hiding, going around in disguise." Marcus nodded with satisfaction, then turned back to Kimberley. "But you don't know any of the groups he played with before?"

"I think there are a couple mentioned in one of the books. I can't remember what their names were." She looked ashamed at having forgotten even the smallest fact about her idol.

"Do you know where we could find out?"

"Oh, yes." She bounced off the bed and went over to a cupboard. "You see, I keep everything I find about the group, but if it's something I don't like, I shove it in here."

She went down on her knees and started shuffling through a pile of newspapers and magazines.

"What do you mean—something you don't like?" asked Stewie.

Kimberley was too busy to hear the question, so Emma supplied the answer. "She means articles which don't think Dazzleman is as wonderful as she does."

"Here it is." Kimberley brandished a page from one of the weekly music papers. "It's rotten, got all the facts wrong, I'm sure, and it's written in a really nasty, sarcastic way."

"Let's have a look." She passed the sheet to Marcus. The other two detectives came close to read the article over his shoulder.

"It's headed THE OLD MAN OF POP." Stewie giggled as he spoke.

Kimberley was furious. "Yes, I know. I told you it was

a rotten article. It really makes him out to be awful. It must have been written by someone who didn't know anything about anything. I mean, to call Dazzleman, who's got to be one of the most talented . . ."

She went on in this way for some time, but the Three Detectives did not listen. They were too busy reading.

*Reddimixx's flamboyant lead singer, Dazzleman, whose appearance at a recent gig had a lot of fans mistaking him for the Tin Man from "The Wizard of Oz," is known to be one of the most secretive rock-stars, and there's one subject he is more sensitive about than any other. His age.*

*The Reddimixx Press Office is happy to pump out any amount of useless rubbish about the superstar's favorite sweets, his taste in clothes, the color of his eyes, and so on. They were even happy to tell me his birth sign (he's a Scorpio, by the way, fans), but when I asked which year was honored by this historic birth, they suddenly went very quiet.*

*I think it would have been better if they'd come right out with it. When you don't know, you start making awful guesses. You start wondering how wrinkled the poor old dear is under all that silver. You start wondering if the head actually is shaved, or if all the hair's just dropped out.*

*Come on, Dazzleman, put us out of our misery. Tell us how old you really are. We can take it.*

*However, I don't think we're likely to get an answer*

*from the silvery pensioner himself, so we have to work it out for ourselves.*

*There is no doubt that Dazzleman has been around the scene a LONG, LONG TIME. Recently someone in the business passed me the photograph printed at the bottom of this column. It dates from 1964, and the group's called Johnny Fann and the Fannfares. According to my informant, the one at the back with the bass guitar and the mophead haircut is none other than Mr. Reddimixx himself.*

*O.K., let's be generous and say the lad was only eighteen at the time. It still mean's he's pushing forty now. Wonder how the teenies would greet that news if it were proved to be true. Eh, Grandad?*

*Come on, the truth can't be as bad as what we're imagining. OWN UP, DAZZLEMAN! HOW OLD ARE YOU?*

When they finished reading, Kimberley was still talking. ". . . and really badly written, apart from anything else. And it's a cheek to say he looks like the Tin Man! I'm surprised newspapers are allowed to print rubbish like that. I mean, honestly . . ."

The Three Detectives continued to ignore her as they looked at the blurred photograph at the foot of the article. On the left was a drummer; on the right, half of a lead guitarist, cut off by the edge of the photograph so that his face was not visible. And in the middle was the figure who might be Dave Smith. All wore neat suits and

Beatle haircuts. In the blurred photograph, each of them could have been anyone. To guess how the middle one would have looked with shaven head, silver make-up, and stick-on mirrors was impossible.

"Still, maybe it's a lead," said Marcus. "At least it's the only lead we've got on what Dazzleman did before Reddimixx."

"Yes," said Stewie ruefully. "If only we had a way of getting in touch with someone who used to play with Johnny Fann and the Fannfares . . ."

"Do you know," Emma announced, "I believe we have?"

☆ ☆ ☆ **11** ☆ ☆ ☆

# Johnny Fann and the Fannfares

Emma could tell from her father's expression when he got in that evening that he hadn't spent the day having wonderful ideas for his television program. He had the tired look of someone who had been trying to have ideas all day and not getting anywhere.

She waited until he was sitting down with a drink before she raised the subject. "Daddy, you know you were trying to think of good names to follow up for this show . . ."

"Yes. And I still can't think of anyone original."

"No ideas at all?"

"No ideas that're worth having. Oh yes, plenty of names spring to mind, but they're all so obvious."

"Well, Daddy, you know I said I'd try and think of some people for you . . ."

He smiled across at her with the infuriating smile parents use when they're being patronizing.

80

"Yes, love, I remember."

"I've had an idea."

"Good for you. They're all welcome." But he still didn't look as if he expected her to come up with anything useful.

Emma began carefully. She didn't want to tell any lies, but on the other hand she didn't want to tell her father the full reason for her interest. "It started from me thinking about Dazzleman."

Douglas Cobbett put his hands to his head in mock-despair. "Don't mention that name to me."

"No, but listen. I was thinking—what about the time before he became Dazzleman? Now he's an international superstar, but there must have been people who worked with him before. If you could get some of those together, you'd have the makings of a really interesting show."

Douglas Cobbett nodded. "You're right, Emma." Now he was taking her seriously. "It would make a smashing program. The only trouble is, love, that there's nothing to go on. Someone mentioned the idea in the office a few days ago, and the researchers did a little preliminary work to see if they could find out anything. And they drew a blank. Yes, Dazzleman must have had a past, but nobody seems to know anything about it. The researchers I've got on this show are the best, but even they can't get anywhere if they haven't got something to start from."

"Say they had the name of a group who Dazzleman used to play with. . . ?"

"If they had that, Emma, there'd be no stopping

them. They'd have tracked down any surviving members of the band within a couple of days."

A little smile tickled the corners of Emma's mouth. "I've been doing a bit of research, too, Daddy."

"Have you, love? And what have you managed to unearth?" But his smile had become patronizing again.

"I know the name of a group that Dazzleman is supposed to have played with back in 1964."

Douglas Cobbett sat up so sharply he almost spilled his drink. "What! Who were they?"

"They were called Johnny Fann and the Fannfares. Do you think your researchers could track down any of the members of the group now they've got the name?"

"Yes, Emma. They most certainly could!"

The Three Detectives met again the next afternoon in Marcus's den. It seemed the most convenient place. There were never any brothers and sisters and rarely any parents to interrupt them. And Kirsten was always on hand, to supply drinks and crisps at her master's command.

"Do you think we'll get anything on Johnny Fann and the Fannfares?" he asked Emma.

"I'm sure we will. The trouble is, though, it may not get us any nearer the truth about Dazzleman. After all, that article didn't say he *definitely* played with the band; it just said someone *suggested* he had."

Marcus nodded. "So we shouldn't count on getting anything from that. We ought to be thinking of other approaches."

"Like getting into Pegler's Hall?" suggested Emma eagerly.

Marcus calmed her with a wave of his hand. "In time, in time. I was thinking of a bit more background research."

Emma snorted. They both knew what she thought of background research. Marcus went on, "I'm going to have another listen to all of the Reddimixx music. I've got a feeling there may be another clue in one of the songs and I'm missing something terribly obvious."

"Will you have to borrow the albums from Kimberley again?"

"No. I'm not daft. I copied them on to cassette that day she lent them to me." He turned to Stewie. "Have you got any ideas of things you might want to follow up?"

The younger boy nodded. "As a matter of fact, I have."

"Going to tell us what it is?"

Stewie shook his head. As with his inventions, he never liked talking about things until they were finished.

"O.K., then," said Marcus. "Let's break up now, shall we? And report back if any of us comes up with anything. O.K.?"

They all agreed to do that, and Emma and Stewie left the house.

As soon as they had gone, Marcus put on one of the cassettes he had copied from Kimberley's albums, plugged in his earphones, and began to listen intently.

Stewie went down to the local library, found where the

telephone directories were kept, and started to work methodically through the Yellow Pages.

And Emma went home to find that her father had news for her.


"You were right," Douglas Cobbett announced as she came in. "A Dave Smith *did* play with Johnny Fann and the Fannfares—and he was definitely the same Dave Smith who later turned himself into Dazzleman."

"That's great!"

"I told you my researchers were good. What's more, they have actually managed to track down one of the original members of the band."

"Terrific! Is he still working as a musician?"

"No. Couldn't be doing anything more different. After Johnny Fann and the Fannfares split up, he learned a craft as a model-maker. You'd never guess in a thousand years what he's doing now."

"What?"

"He runs a dolls' hospital."

"A dolls' hospital! What, you mean to mend old dolls that have got broken?"

"Exactly that."

"But that's good, isn't it? It'll give you something really interesting to film when you talk to him. It'll make a wonderful program!"

"Yes." Douglas Cobbett sighed. "It would have."

"Would have?"

"We can't do it, love, I'm afraid. It was a smashing idea of yours, but we can't do it."

"Why ever not?"

"Because the man in question refuses to talk about the group on television."

"Why?"

Douglas Cobbett shrugged. "No idea. But he's quite definite that he won't. One of the researchers got through to him on the phone, and he admitted that he used to be bass guitarist with Johnny Fann and the Fannfares, but when she told him about the television series, he just shut up. Wouldn't say any more."

"And he gave no reason?"

"None at all. I thought maybe he was only saying that because the girl was just a researcher, so I rang him myself. I thought perhaps he'd listen to the program's producer. But no. He still refused to be on the program."

"What did he actually say?"

"I remember his words quite clearly. He said, 'No, that's all over. Johnny Fann and the Fannfares don't exist anymore. We don't want to dig up the past.'"

"I wonder why. Most people are delighted at the chance of being on television."

"I know, it's very strange." Douglas Cobbett shook his head slowly. "And do you know, Emma, the strangest thing of all was that when he spoke to me about the group, he sounded sort of . . ."

"Sort of what, Daddy?"

"Frightened. Very, very frightened."

# ☆ ☆ ☆ 12 ☆ ☆ ☆

# The Dolls' Hospital

On Saturdays, breakfast in the Cobbett household was later than during the rest of the week. Douglas Cobbett and his wife liked to sleep in. Emma herself usually felt little urgency to get up, though how long she could stay in bed depended on how long she could stand Tommy whining that he wanted a drink.

It was therefore quite a surprise that particular Saturday for Mrs. Cobbett (who had sneaked down to the kitchen to make a pot of tea, which she intended to smuggle back upstairs again before Tommy realized she was up) to find her stepdaughter already breakfasted and dressed by eight o'clock, just as if it were a school day.

What made the sight even more surprising was that Emma, who had ceased to play with dolls many years before, was cradling an old porcelain-headed doll called Lily. Lily had first belonged to Emma's great-grandmother. She had then been passed on to Emma's grandmother, then to Emma's mother, and finally to Emma.

The doll had been her pride and joy. As a little girl, Emma had dressed and undressed Lily a hundred times a day and talked to her continuously. But for some years the doll had been left undisturbed in a cupboard with other toys whose moment of popularity was past.

Giving pleasure to four generations of little girls is a great achievement for a doll, but it doesn't do it much good. Little girls tend to express their love robustly, and Lily had suffered a great deal of little girls' love. The result was that, as she approached her hundredth year, Lily looked rather the worse for wear. In her fabric body, under her lacy petticoats and long, trimmed pantaloons, there were tears and splits, through which the horsehair stuffing protruded. Some of her carefully-planted human hair had come out, and on one side, it had even been snipped short where one of her owners had decided to modernize the style with a pair of nail scissors. All the fingers had been broken off one porcelain hand, the nose was chipped, and the painted features of the face almost worn away by childish kisses. Lily had been much-loved, but much-battered.

"What on earth are you doing with Lily?" asked Mrs. Cobbett, yawning and pulling her dressing-gown around her.

"I've heard of a place where I can get her mended," Emma replied. "A dolls' hospital."

"But why, suddenly? You haven't played with her for years."

"No, I just came across her the other day and thought

she looked in need of repair." It was only a half lie. "She is a family treasure, you know."

Mrs. Cobbett shrugged. "Where is this dolls' hospital place?"

"Wandsworth. Only half an hour on the train."

"I still don't see why you suddenly—"

"It's not far. I'll be back by lunchtime. That's why I'm making such an early start."

"Well . . ." Mrs. Cobbett didn't look convinced.

But then the kettle started to whistle. At the same moment Tommy appeared, demanding "a dinkandosandam" (which any member of the family could immediately translate as "a drink and toast and jam"). In the ensuing confusion, Emma got her coat and left the house.

When Mrs. Cobbett finally got back up to the bedroom with her pot of tea (and a very jammy Tommy in tow), she forgot to mention to Douglas where their daughter had gone. He might have seen more than coincidence in Emma's sudden decision to get her doll mended.

At about nine o'clock their rest, already made less pleasant by Tommy wriggling, kicking, and wiping jammy hands all over their faces, was further disturbed by the phone ringing.

It was Marcus, wanting to speak to Emma. He sounded excited. No, sorry, they said, Emma had just gone out. Should be back at lunchtime.

Five minutes later there was another phone call.

This time it was Stewie, sounding equally excited, also asking to speak to Emma. He got the same reply.

Then Marcus rang Stewie. Both of them had been successful in their researches. Each one had discovered a clue to where Dazzleman might be hidden. And both clues pointed to the same hiding-place.

Emma found the dolls' hospital without difficulty. It was about twenty minutes' walk from Wandsworth Town station.

The night before, Douglas Cobbett had shown his daughter the typewritten notes that his researchers had produced in their search for the members of Johnny Fann and the Fannfares. From these Emma had memorized the Wandsworth address.

And the name of the former pop musician who worked there. Eddie Bartlett.

The address proved to be an old shop in a row of four others. None of them looked as if they were doing any business. One was boarded up, two showed a scattered mess of discarded shopfittings. But the dusty window of the fourth was filled with the bodies of dolls.

They were piled right to the ceiling, so that no light could have penetrated through the plate-glass to the interior of the shop. There was an enormous variety of dolls, of all ages and sizes. Old porcelain ones like Lily lay tangled with grinning plastic babies. Sagging rag dolls entwined with dolls in national costumes. Dusty faces peered out through a jungle of grubby, chubby plastic limbs.

And all the dolls were broken. Some had lost an arm or leg. Some were headless, others cracked or dented. Loose limbs, spare torsos, and bodiless heads joined the confusion behind the dusty glass.

The effect was odd, even slightly frightening, and it was a moment before Emma took in the rest of the shop's frontage. When she did, she saw a shabby blue board over the window. On this in black letters was written, DOLLS' CASUALTY WARD. At the side of the window was a door with cracked blue paint. On this was a rusty black knocker. Beside it, almost coming away from the wall, a plastic bell-push. In its little window was a scrap of paper bearing the scribbled name, Bartlett.

Emma took a deep breath and pressed the button. Inside the shop, nothing stirred.

She looked at the upstairs windows, where presumably there was an apartment. Behind the dusty glass, faded curtains were firmly drawn.

She pressed the bell-push again. She waited. One minute. Two minutes. Three. Still there was no sound from inside the shop.

Oh, dear. Had she come all this way to find no one at home? Maybe Eddie Bartlett didn't work on Saturdays. Maybe he didn't live on the premises. The television researchers had only supplied the one address, but it was quite possible that he had a home a long way away from his work. She wondered if she would have to check out all of the E. Bartletts in the London telephone directory. She didn't fancy the idea. Apart from the fact that research bored her, Bartlett was a common name and it could be a long job.

It was then she had the thought that perhaps the bell wasn't working. Coming away from the wall like that, it might well have a broken connection. Certainly when she pressed it, she could hear no answering buzz from inside.

She tried the knocker. The noise was surprisingly loud in the quiet street as she gave three hard bangs on the door.

Again there was silence. Angry at the failure of her mission, she was about to stump back to the railway station when she did hear a little sound.

There was movement inside the shop. The movement drew closer. The door opened.

The man who stood there looked small and unwell. His hair was shaggy and could have done with a wash. In his thin, lined face, sunken black eyes burned. He wore a soiled, once-white apron over faded jeans and a pullover the color of school gravy.

The little eyes did not seem to see Emma. They moved straight to the doll clasped in her arms. His thin hands went toward it, and without thinking, Emma found herself handing Lily over.

An expression of tenderness came into the man's voice as he cradled the doll in his arms. "Oh, who's a beauty?" he crooned, in a soft voice. "You really have got a lovely one there. Genuine Victorian, she is. Suffering a bit from old age, but we can sort her out, don't worry."

"You really think you can?" asked Emma. "I mean, one of her hands is broken."

"That's no problem. I'll find one to match." He indicated the tangled pile of dolls in the window. "There'll be something in there. I keep those for spares, you know." He looked at Emma for the first time, with a glint of humor in his eyes. "Why, were you worried that I had to work through all that lot before I got 'round to mending your little darling?"

Emma grinned. "I suppose I had thought that, yes."

"Come in." The man beckoned. "Let's take a look and see how serious the damage really is."

If from the outside the shop had given the impression of hundreds of dolls, the inside gave the impression of thousands. There were ceiling-high shelves on all three sides of the room. And on every shelf there were more dolls—dolls looking extremely ill, dolls half-mended who were looking better, dolls who had completed their treatment and whose newly-painted cheeks glowed with health.

In the middle of the room was a large table. This was littered with odd limbs and eyes and scraps of dolls' hair. There were pots of paint and glue scattered amid brushes, knives, chisels, needles, and reels of thread.

Eddie Bartlett cleared a space with one hand and laid Lily down. He handled her gently, as if he were indeed a doctor and she a real sick child. He moved a lamp down closer over the small body and examined her injuries. As he did so, he kept up a flow of talk in a strange, gentle voice.

"She's really old, you know. Beautiful craftsmanship. What's her name? Lily, eh? That's a good name. Has she been in your family long? Your great-grandmother had her? Well, we must really do something for her, mustn't we? A grand old lady like Lily must look her best. You leave her with me and I'll make her look exactly as she did when your great-grandmother opened the box over a hundred years ago, Good as new, she'll be. Better. I'll put a happier expression on her face. Only thing I have against these Victorian dolls—they always look a bit solemn. But don't worry, I can remedy that. She'll have to be laid up for a few days, poor old lady, but soon she'll be her old self again."

"How long will it take?" asked Emma. It wasn't really the question she wanted to ask. Somehow she had to move the conversation around to the real subject of her visit, but it was difficult to make such an abrupt change.

"Oh, give me a week and she'll be right as rain," Eddie Bartlett replied. "Yes, come back this time next week and you can pick up a very beautiful lady."

"And what will it cost?" she asked, still trying to think of ways of getting around to the subject of Johnny Fann and the Fannfares.

Eddie Bartlett's sharp eyes looked into hers. "Who'll be paying?" he asked. "Your Mum and Dad? Or is it going to have to come out of your pocket money?"

"I'll pay. She is my doll."

Eddie Bartlett nodded, as if pleased by the answer. "It'll cost you two pounds," he said.

"Only two pounds? That seems awfully cheap."

"Two pounds is the price. It would have been more if your parents were paying."

"But I don't want you to be losing money over—"

Eddie Bartlett's finger to his lips stopped her. "Two pounds. Don't argue. There aren't that many bargains in this life. When you see one, you ought to grab it straight away."

"All right." Emma grinned. "Thank you very much."

Eddie reached into the piles on the table for a scrap of paper and a three-inch stub of pencil. "Now, I'd better get your name and telephone number. Then I can let you know if there's any problems. Shouldn't be, but it's best to be sure."

"My name is Emma Cobbett."

The pencil hovered in the air for a moment, hesitating, before he wrote the surname down.

And when Emma gave her phone number, he stopped writing and looked at her with an expression of puzzlement on his face.

"Yesterday," he began slowly, "somebody else gave me that phone number. A television producer called Douglas Cobbett. He gave me his office number and his home number, and said I mustn't hesitate to call him if I changed my mind about . . . about something."

The black eyes seemed to be drilling into her, as Emma gulped and said, "Douglas Cobbett is my father."

The gentleness had gone from Eddie Bartlett's voice in his next question. "Why are you really here, Emma Cobbett?"

"I want to talk about Johnny Fann and the Fannfares."

At the mention of the name, there was no doubt that the expression in Eddie Bartlett's eyes was one of fear.

# 13

# The Death of a Pop Musician

When Eddie Bartlett next spoke, there was anger, as well as fear, in his voice. "Your father's got a nerve. I told him quite definitely there was no way I was going to appear on his lousy television program. But he just can't take no for an answer, can he? I've heard of some shabby tricks in my time, but I think using his daughter to come 'round and persuade me is the shabbiest of the lot. I suppose this doll isn't even yours. All that business about your great-grandmother was a load of lies. Your father just bought this as a means of getting you in to see me."

"No, he didn't! I promise he didn't! Lily really was my great-grandmother's. And my grandmother's. And my mother's. You must believe me."

He seemed for a moment to be calmed by this, but then the anger flared again. "Still, jolly convenient for your father, wasn't it—to have the doll lying 'round the house. I think it's disgusting. It's not your fault, but I'm sorry for you—sorry you have a father who'd descend to this sort of trick."

"He would never do that!" Emma protested. "You've misunderstood completely."

"Oh, have I?"

"Yes, you have. My father doesn't even know I'm here!"

Eddie Bartlett looked straight into her eyes for a long moment. Something he saw in them must have convinced him she was telling the truth. Some of the anger went from his face, but suspicion remained. "All right, I believe you. But if your father has nothing to do with it, why are you here? I'm afraid I'm not going to believe it's pure coincidence that I suddenly hear one day from Douglas Cobbett wanting to talk about Johnny Fann and the Fannfares, and the next morning Emma Cobbett turns up to talk about exactly the same subject."

"No, it's not coincidence," Emma admitted. "I did get your name and address from my father's research." She saw the light of suspicion grow in Eddie's eyes and hurried on. "But I'm not interested in the television program. And my father's not trying to make you change your mind. I talked to him last night about it, and he has accepted that you won't do the program. He's sorry, because he thinks it would make a good show, but he accepts your decision."

"If that's so," Eddie asked slowly, "then why are you

here? Why do you want to know about Johnny Fann and the Fannfares?" A look of mild disgust came into his face. "Oh, no, you're not just another mad Dazzleman fan who wants to find out about—"

"No, no, I'm not," Emma assured him.

"Then, once again, I ask—why are you here?"

Emma took a deep breath. She had decided that, as usual, honesty was going to be the best policy.

"It is about Dazzleman, yes, but I'm not here just because I am a fan. As you've probably seen in the papers, he's disappeared."

"That's a little habit of his," said Eddie Bartlett, as if bored by the whole subject.

"Yes, but this time I think he may not have disappeared because he wanted to, but because someone else wanted him to."

"You mean you think he's been murdered?"

"No, not that. But I think he may have been kidnapped."

"Where on earth did you get that idea?"

Briefly Emma outlined the events in the studio on the day of Dazzleman's disappearance, the strange autograph, and the song to which it was the key. "*You Can Set Me Free,* it's called," she concluded. "I don't know if you know it?"

He nodded. "Yes. I know it. I've known it for a long time. Hmm. That's all very ingenious, tying in the message and the song like that, but it could just be coincidence. I'd want rather more definite proof before I believed that Dave had actually been kidnapped."

"The other strange thing about it is the timing of his disappearance. In the middle of making the video, before the final mix of the single's been agreed . . ."

Eddie's attitude changed. "Yes, that is odd. Dave was always very shrewd. I mean, twenty years ago, when we were in the band, he used to have his moods. He didn't shoot off abroad, like he does now—couldn't afford to in those days—but he would still throw scenes, have little fits of temperament. But even then they were always carefully timed. He'd never actually ruin anything important that we'd got coming up. He was always on time for the gigs, that sort of thing."

"Anyway, that's why I've come to see you," said Emma. "I think he has been kidnapped, and I think the reason for it may be some secret in his past. That's why I want to know about Johnny Fann and the Fannfares."

"There were a good few secrets in Dave's past, certainly." Eddie gave a short laugh. Then he seemed suddenly to turn gloomy. "I'm away from all that now. It's twenty years ago. After the terrible . . . after Johnny Fann and the Fannfares split up, I got out of the pop business completely. Did a lot of other things, then sort of drifted into craftwork, and at last"—he indicated the shelves of dolls around him—"found what I really wanted to do."

"And you never wanted to get back into music?"

He shook his head firmly. "Never. That part of my life was over. I didn't want to think about it. Still don't want to think about it."

In spite of his words, his thoughts seemed to be going

99

back, so Emma gently prompted him, "What sort of a group was Johnny Fann and the Fannfares?"

There was another little laugh. "A pretty bad group, I think, if the truth were told."

"How many were you?"

"Four. Almost all the groups were four then. The Beatles were the biggest thing to have hit pop music for years, and all the other groups copied them. Three guitars and a drummer—that was the line-up they wanted. Try anything else and you wouldn't get any bookings."

"What did you play?"

"I was bass guitar. Then there was Dave—Dazzleman, as he now is—on rhythm. Terry Walton lead guitar, and on drums we had . . . we had a bloke called Dusty Ellis."

"So who was Johnny Fann?"

"Ah, of course, yes. Johnny Fann. Well, in those days—and now too, come to that—the first thing you did when you started a group was to get a name. Very few people used their own names. Johnny Fann and the Fannfares seemed silly enough for the time. Johnny Fann himself was Terry Walton—he did most of the vocals, him and Dave, anyway. He was the sort of front man for the group—you know, he was bigger than the rest of us, looked good standing up by the microphone."

"And what kind of music did you play?"

"All sorts. We weren't very good, you know, just learning. We were based in Manchester, played clubs, church halls 'round there mostly. Only semiprofessional, really. Dusty was still a student. The rest of us did other odd jobs . . . But, as for what we played . . . well, you'd do your version of all the latest hits, you'd play a few oldies—even try some of our own songs."

"You wrote your own?"

"I didn't. I couldn't do it to save my life. No, Terry and Dave did the writing. Some of the numbers weren't half bad. They'd got a good sense of melody, those two. Well, I say two, but I think it was only one who could really do it."

"What do you mean?"

"They used to go off, Terry and Dave, to have these writing sessions, and then they'd come back, and say they'd written the songs together. I think it was a bit like Lennon and McCartney—I don't know if you know, all the Beatles songs were supposed to be written by both of them, but in fact they had different styles and you can always recognize a song that's *mostly* John Lennon or *mostly* Paul McCartney. I reckon it was the same with Dave and Terry—the only difference between them and the Beatles being that one of them was good and the other wasn't."

In reply to Emma's puzzled expression, Eddie went on, "I mean, they'd come back with these songs that they said they'd written together, but we could tell the difference in them. One of them wrote really great songs, and the other wrote really dull ones."

"And who wrote the good ones?"

"Dave. Obviously. I say 'obviously,' because a lot of the numbers he's done with Reddimixx were first played by Johnny Fann and the Fannfares. They sound a bit different—the backing's all electronic, the lyrics have been changed a bit—but they're basically the same numbers. And they've all got Dave's name on them as composer, so he must have been the good one and Terry the dull one."

"That's very interesting," said Emma.

Eddie Bartlett looked at her sharply. "Maybe it is, but understand this—it doesn't go any farther than these four walls. I don't want the press nosing about. I don't want television producers like your father doing programs about it."

"All right. I'll keep it quiet. I just think it's an interesting story—and one that the public would like to know about."

"Well, they're not going to know about it," Eddie snapped. Then, in a more thoughtful tone, he continued, "Some things are better kept quiet. There's nothing to be gained by stirring up the past."

"What happened, Eddie?" asked Emma gently.

"Happened? When?"

"Something happened while you were with Johnny Fann and the Fannfares. Something you don't want to talk about. Something that frightens you."

"You're talking rubbish!" He moved abruptly toward the door. "I think you'd better go now."

Emma didn't move. "Well, if you won't tell me, I suppose I'll just have to find out from one of the other members of the group."

Eddie Bartlett laughed harshly. "You'll be lucky."

"I don't see why you say that. If Daddy's researchers could track you down, I'm sure they could do the same for the rest of the group."

"They might find that more difficult. Listen." And, as he mentioned the names, Eddie counted them off on his fingers. "Dave . . . as you know well, Dave has disappeared. So's Terry Walton—except he disappeared even longer ago. Our Terry hasn't been seen since 1965. And Dusty . . . Dusty . . ." His voice broke.

"What about Dusty? Where's he?"

Eddie had regained control, but his voice was dull as he replied. "Dusty is in a cemetery on the outskirts of Manchester. Dusty died in 1965."

"And is that why the band split up?"

He nodded.

"And why you left the music business?"

Another nod.

From nowhere, like a flash of lightning, a thought came into Emma's head. "And was that why Terry Walton disappeared?"

"Yes," Eddie replied wearily. "That was why."

"What actually *did* happen?"

Eddie Bartlett began to speak. It was as if Emma were not there. He sounded as if he were speaking to himself, painfully digging out long-buried memories.

"We'd got a one-night stand booked at a club in Sal-

103

ford. Quite a rough place it was, but we weren't well-known, we couldn't afford to be choosy. We just needed work, so we took bookings anywhere. Terry and Dusty had never really got on, not from the time we started the group. They were always arguing, about everything. They didn't agree about the music the band should be playing, they didn't agree about the bookings we should take, they didn't agree about the clothes we should wear. They didn't agree about anything.

"But that night in Salford, things were worse than ever between them. Terry had this girlfriend, see, name of Caroline. They'd been going around for a long time . . . I don't know, over a year maybe. And at the beginning of the evening, before we started playing, this Caroline gives Terry the Big E—do you know what I mean when I say that?"

Emma nodded.

"But that's not all of it. She doesn't just say that she's not going out with Terry anymore, she tells him the reason. And that reason is that she's going to go out with Dusty instead. Well, like I said, the two of them weren't great buddies at the best of times, but this latest thing really puts the cat among the pigeons. We somehow get through playing the music, you know, doing what we was paid for, but there's real hate flowing between Terry and Dusty. It's bound to lead to trouble, and it does. As soon as we have a break, they start shouting at each other, and when we finally stop playing, there's no holding them. They go out into the car-park."

"To fight?"

"That's it. To have a fight, yes. The whole thing's total confusion. I said it was a pretty rough crowd there—a lot of them hadn't liked our music, anyway—and when they hear there's going to be a fight, most of the lads who've been dancing rush out to the car-park to see what's going on. Dave and me stay inside the hall, packing up the speakers and what-have-you, and we can hear all this shouting going on outside, and we don't know what we should do, whether we should try to interfere, whether it's better just to let them get on with it.

"And then it all goes quiet.

"We think it's strange. After all, there were so many people out there and then suddenly it's gone quiet. We hear a few cars driving off, a few motorbikes, and then this total silence. After a few minutes we go out.

"And do you know, there's not a living soul in that whole car-park. They've all gone, vanished, just like that.

"And then, as we're looking 'round, we nearly fall over Dusty. He's lying there, in a puddle, and he's been stabbed in the chest with a sheath knife. He's dead.

"Well, we call the police and they come, and over the next few days they round up all the people who were at the dance that night, and two of the blokes tell them they saw Terry and Dusty fighting. And they say they saw Terry take out a knife and stab Dusty—and that's why they all ran off so quickly."

"Did Terry always carry a knife?" asked Emma.

105

"Not that I knew of." Eddie shrugged. "But he must've done, mustn't he?"

"I suppose so. And he was never seen again?"

"No. You see, it was a couple of days after the murder that these witnesses came forward. That had given Terry time to get away. He went abroad. The police traced him down to Dover and found out he'd taken a ferry to France two days before they got there. Since then, no one's seen him."

"It must have been terrible for you."

Eddie nodded grimly. "Yes. Perhaps you understand now why I didn't want to talk on your father's television program. Perhaps you understand now why I gave up the music business and"—he picked up Lily and looked into her faded eyes—"found something more peaceful."

"Yes. I do understand."

"And if the story of Dazzleman's past ever gets out to the papers, Emma," he looked at her directly as he spoke her name, "I'll know who to blame."

"You can trust me. And thank you for telling me."

He sighed. "Quite a relief to tell someone, really. It's the kind of thing you never forget. Talking helps."

"Good."

He was still holding Lily, and he thrust the doll toward her owner. "I suppose you'll want to take this back, now you've found out what you're after."

"Oh no," said Emma. "I really would like to have her mended. Really. If you don't mind."

"No, I don't mind. Mended she shall be." He looked

106

again into the doll's face, and his expression became more tender.

Emma rose. "Thank you for talking to me. I suppose I'd better be going. I said I'd be back for lunch."

He nodded, exhausted by the tale he had told.

"Oh, one thing. . . ," said Emma.

He looked up at her.

"You haven't, by any chance, got a picture of the group, have you? Of Johnny Fann and the Fannfares?"

He grinned ruefully. "Yes, I think I have somewhere. Excuse me a minute."

He went out into the back of the shop and returned a few minutes later with an old, dusty photograph. "It's one of the few. Not many taken of us, I'm afraid. We never got to the stage of record contracts and publicity photographs and all that. Perhaps we would have"—he shrugged—"if things had turned out differently."

She took the photograph from his outstretched hand. It was the same one that had appeared in Kimberley's music paper, but that had only showed part of the picture, focusing on Dave Smith. This one showed all four members of the band.

There was Dusty, the dead drummer, on the left, and next to him the man who was to become Dazzleman. On the far right, plumper and healthier-looking, but still recognizable, was Eddie Bartlett.

But it was the figure in the middle who took Emma's breath away. He was the tall lead guitarist who had been cut in half in the newspaper photograph.

107

Terry Walton. Dusty Ellis's murderer.

But Emma knew him by a different name.

Like the rest of the group, the lead guitarist wore a mophead Beatle haircut. He had no beard. And his face was younger.

But Emma Cobbett had no doubts that it was a photograph of the man who now called himself Stick.

# 14

# The Three Detectives Make Plans

Emma got home just in time for lunch, but she had little appetite. Her mind was working too fast for her to be hungry. It kept reorganizing the information she had received in the dolls' hospital that morning, making new and frightening patterns.

Under normal circumstances, her parents might have noticed that she was not eating and started to ask awkward questions. But fortunately Tommy was being at his most destructive, and Mr. and Mrs. Cobbett hardly noticed what Emma was doing. Tommy had just discovered that, by balancing a spoonful of food on the edge of his plate and banging the handle down, he could make a very effective catapult. His parents were kept busy persuading him that this was a bad idea and fielding the lumps of mashed potato that he did manage to launch while they weren't watching.

After lunch, Emma rushed upstairs to the telephone in her parents' room. She needed to contact the other two detectives urgently.

They were equally keen to talk to her, and so Marcus and Stewie arranged to go to Emma's house. Normally they'd have met at Marcus's, but his parents were paying one of their rare visits home and had organized a tennis party. Marcus knew that, if he stayed around, he would be forced onto the tennis court, and that idea was so appalling to him that he was very glad to have the chance to get out.

Also, Emma was going to be on her own at home, which was another good thing, from the point of view of secrecy. Mr. and Mrs. Cobbett had managed to ignore for some time the fact that Tommy had grown out of all his shoes, but that morning he had managed to cut through his last remaining pair of sandals with a kitchen knife. This meant that they could not escape taking him to the shoe shop. Fitting Tommy with a new pair of shoes (or at least keeping him in one place while he was fitted with a pair of shoes) was a task that required the full strength of both parents, and if Emma hadn't refused very firmly, she too would have been dragged along as extra musclepower.

Marcus and Stewie arrived full of excitement.

"I think we've really got somewhere," said Marcus. "Where were you this morning? We rang you."

"I was out on Three Detectives business, don't worry. And I think you could say that I got somewhere, too."

"Terrific. So we've all got something to report."

"Who's going to go first?" asked Stewie.

"I don't mind," said Marcus. "What I've found out is so obvious, I feel almost ashamed of it. Not ashamed because it's not good—just ashamed because I should have got there earlier.

"You know I said I was going to go through all the Reddimixx music again? Well, I did, you know, to see if there were any clues that we'd missed. And I found one straight away, staring me in the face."

"In which song?" asked Emma.

"In the song that the autograph pointed to. *You Can Set Me Free*. We really should have listened to the lyric of that more closely. It's so obvious."

"Stop saying it's obvious and tell me what's obvious!"

"All right, Emma. Keep your hair on. Look, I've written the lyric out." He handed over the sheet of paper. "Stewie knows about it. Can you see anything?"

Emma glanced at the lyric. The words were familiar from the time they had listened for the first clue, but she could not at first see anything more in them.

"First verse," Marcus prompted. "Right at the beginning. Take it literally."

Emma started to read the words out. As she did so, the truth dawned on her.

*"I'm in trouble.*
*All alone.*
*I'm like a prisoner*
*In my own home.*

*Only you*—Oh, my goodness! Of course. 'I'm like a prisoner in my own home'. 'In my own home!' That's what you meant, wasn't it?"

"Yes."

"Dazzleman's being held inside his own home! At Pegler's Hall!"

"That's what I reckon. And what Stewie's found out seems to support the idea."

Emma turned to look at Stewie. He scratched his muddle of hair before he spoke. "You see, Emma, I'd been thinking through everything we saw when we paid our visit to Pegler's End. I had a feeling there must be some important detail that we had forgotten, something we may have noticed at the time, but didn't think was important. I racked my brains and after a long time I could only come up with one thing."

"What was that?"

"Do you remember, as we were leaving the gates, just after Stick had told me to scram, and just before Bill came out, a delivery van went through the gates?"

"Yes."

"And it had a name on the side."

"Yes." Emma screwed up her eyes as she tried to bring the picture back into her mind. "Sparks, was it? Or Shanks? Something beginning with S, I'm sure."

"J. Spink & Sons," Stewie announced calmly.

"That was it."

"Well, once I'd remembered it, I thought I'd try and find out what the van was delivering. It might, of course, have been something perfectly ordinary, or it might be something that was going to give us some kind of clue.

"So I went to the library and checked in the Yellow Pages. It didn't take long to find them—they're a local firm. J. Spink & Sons are fishmongers, rather high-class fishmongers."

"So?" asked Emma.

"So I thought I'd better find out what they were delivering to Pegler's Hall."

"How did you do that?"

"I went to see Kimberley."

"Kimberley!" Emma was astonished. "What on earth would she know about anything?"

"You forget," said Stewie gently, "that Kimberley's mother owns a restaurant. People who own restaurants know all the local suppliers of meat and vegetables—and fish."

"Of course."

"And we were lucky. It turned out that Mrs. Dolan did a lot of business with J. Spink & Sons. In fact, they supply all the fish for the restaurant. And Tony Spink is a particular friend of hers."

"Tony Spink?"

"He's one of the '& Sons,'" Stewie explained. "At this point I'm afraid I had to tell a bit of a lie. You see, I got to talking to Kim about Dazzleman's favorite food."

"Lobster," Emma murmured. She was beginning to see the direction in which Stewie was heading.

"Yes. And I said to Kim, wouldn't it be fun to find out

113

how much lobster Dazzleman ate . . . you know, what the regular order to Pegler's Hall was, how often it was delivered, that sort of thing. She thought it was a fantastic idea, and she asked her mother to ask Tony."

"Well done, Stewie. Kim is so mad on Dazzleman, she'd do anything to find out the tiniest detail about him."

"Exactly. So we went to Kim's Mum and asked. She thought it was a bit funny, but she didn't mind. I think she always does more or less what Kim wants, anyway, and since Tony was a special friend of hers . . ."

"So what did she find out?"

"There is a regular daily order to Pegler's Hall of two fresh lobsters. Sometimes, if there are a lot of people staying, the order goes up, but that's the basic one. And someone rings from the house once a week to confirm that order and add any extras. If Dazzleman's away on tour or something, the order is cancelled."

"And since Dazzleman disappeared this time?"

"He's been gone two weeks. Both weeks the call has come from the house confirming the order."

Emma's cheeks glowed with excitement. "That must mean he's in there!"

"Not necessarily." Marcus could at times be maddeningly calm. "It could be other people in the house who are eating the lobsters."

"No, it couldn't," Emma retorted. "Because there aren't any other people in the house. Stick gave them all the Big E."

"What about Stick himself? Maybe he sits down every night and gorges himself on two whole lobsters."

"I'm positive he doesn't."

"I don't know how you can be so sure, Emma."

"I can be so sure, Marcus, because I know that Stick is a vegetarian! I remember Bill said so the day of the filming."

This silenced Marcus's objections. "So that would seem to mean," he said slowly, "that Dazzleman is being kept, as the song says, like a prisoner in his own home. And the only person who can be keeping him there is Stick. But Stick didn't kidnap him. He wasn't driving the car that took Dazzleman away, was he?"

"No, he wasn't." Emma closed her eyes and tried to see again that sunny afternoon in the studio car-park, tried to imagine herself sitting on the wall with her book, to see the Rolls-Royce draw up, to see Dazzleman come out of the studio, to see the anxiety in his eyes, to see him come toward her . . . *"I've got it!"* she shrieked.

"What?" asked Marcus and Stewie together.

"I know what was odd about Dazzleman leaving the studio. You know I said he walked out as if he didn't really want to, and he looked afraid . . ."

"Yes." Again they spoke together.

"Well, I've also remembered that he kept looking behind him, looking nervously back to the studio door."

"Maybe he was afraid someone would come out and try to stop him getting away," suggested Marcus.

Emma shook her head. "No, he wasn't looking back

115

for someone trying to *stop* him get away—he was looking back at the person who was *making* him go away."

"I don't understand."

"I'm sure Stick was standing in the shadows just inside the door. And I'm sure Stick had a gun pointing right at Dazzleman."

"A gun?"

"Yes. That's why Dazzleman was moving as if he didn't want to. That's why he looked so frightened. That's why he got into the car without making any fuss. And it's also why he wrote the autograph for me. He couldn't raise the alarm any other way without risking being shot, so he gave me the message and hoped that I would work it out."

"Which, fortunately, we did," said Marcus. He paused for a moment. "Yes, it does seem to make sense. Only one thing . . . do you think Stick is really the sort to threaten someone with a gun?"

"Yes," said Emma grimly. "I'm rather afraid he is."

And she told them all that she had found out from Eddie Bartlett in the dolls' hospital that morning. When she finished, the other two faces were as grim as hers.

"So," said Marcus, "that means that the person we are dealing with is a murderer."

"Yes." Then Stewie voiced the worry that they all felt. "I do hope Dazzleman's all right."

Marcus rubbed his chin thoughtfully. "I should think he's all right at the moment. The continuing order for lobsters suggests that he's still alive, anyway—and being

116

treated fairly well, come to that. But Stick's a violent man and Dazzleman's in serious danger."

"Now," said Emma decisively, "we've just got to get inside Pegler's Hall and find out what's going on." She couldn't resist adding, "As I've been saying *for days,* Marcus."

"All right, I know you have. And now I admit that does seem to be what has to be done. But how? We've seen the place. We know what the security's like. Getting in there is not going to be easy."

"I think I know how we could do it," said Stewie quietly.

The other two looked at him in surprise as he went on. "I've been racking my brains since we went to Pegler's End, and I think I have now worked out a way of doing it. I got the idea while I was 'round at Kimberley's. In fact, she really showed me how to do it."

"Kimberley did?" asked Emma in disbelief.

"Well, Kimberley sort of helped. And her mother helped. Though I don't think either of them realized at the time that that was what they were doing. You remember I said that Mrs. Dolan got all her fish from J. Spink & Sons?"

"Yes."

"Well, that has to be delivered, doesn't it? And I found out from Mrs. Dolan when it gets delivered. She gets her week's supply late on a Tuesday afternoon."

"So what?" asked Marcus.

"Wait, and I'll explain. I also managed to find out that

that is the last-but-one of Tuesday's regular deliveries for the van. And the last delivery of the day," Stewie concluded triumphantly, "is to Pegler's Hall."

"I think I see what you're getting at," said Emma excitedly. "You mean that the driver should arrive at the Green Parrot on Tuesday afternoon with a load of fish for the restaurant, and while he's delivering it, we should sneak into the back of the van. . . ?"

Stewie nodded.

A big grin spread over Marcus's chubby face. "So that when the van arrives at Pegler's Hall and is let in through the gates, it contains two lobsters and Three Detectives."

"Yes." Stewie hesitated. "Well, not quite, actually. I'm afraid to get the information I needed I had to tell Kimberley about the idea. And she would only help if I agreed to let her come, too. So I'm afraid when the van arrives at Pegler's Hall, it's going to contain two lobsters, Three Detectives—and Kimberley."

"Oh, dear," said Emma and Marcus.

# ☆ ☆ ☆ 15 ☆ ☆ ☆

# The Break-In

Though they didn't want to have Kimberley with them for their adventure, the Three Detectives couldn't have managed it without her. She knew exactly when and where J. Spink & Sons' delivery van would arrive, and hid her friends so that they could climb into it when the moment came.

The Green Parrot restaurant faced the High Street, in the middle of a parade of shops. 'Round the back, where one might have expected a garden in an ordinary house, there was a small yard with double gates opening on to the road behind. It was here that all the deliveries to the restaurant were made.

The yard itself was small. A ground-floor extension from the main building ran along one side; this was the restaurant's kitchen and storage-room, where the deep-freezes were kept. Along the other side were a couple of small sheds, containing extra tables, broken chairs, boxes of spare glasses, old Christmas decorations, and other oddments.

It was into one of these sheds that Kimberley led the Three Detectives after school on Tuesday afternoon. "It's all right," she said, as she closed the door behind them. "Mum's doing the flowers in the front of the restaurant, so she won't have seen us."

"Where does she think you are?" asked Emma.

"I told her I'm with you. Which is true."

Marcus consulted his watch. "Now what time do you expect the van to arrive?"

"It's usually here 'round five."

"And how long does it stay?"

"That depends who's driving. If it's just one of the ordinary drivers, he's only here as long as it takes to unload the fish and put it in the freezer. If Tony Spink himself comes, he'll be here longer."

"What do you mean?" asked Marcus.

"Well, I told you he's a friend of Mum's. I think he rather fancies her, actually. Anyway, if he comes, he always goes in and they have a drink together. He usually stays about half an hour."

"Let's hope it's him today," said Emma. "Then we'll have more time to get into the van."

"Yes."

There was a silence, which Stewie's voice broke. "Are you really going to wear *that*, Kim?"

"Why not?" She looked defensive, daring the others to criticize her clothes.

Emma and Marcus looked at her. She was wearing another of her Dazzleman sweatshirts. This one was electric blue. The whole of the front was covered with glitter, in the middle of which the word "Dazzleman" was picked out in gold.

"It is a bit conspicuous," said Emma. The Three Detectives were all wearing dark sweaters over their school uniforms.

Surprisingly, Marcus did not object to the sweatshirt. "It may not be a bad idea to wear it. Makes us look as if we're just Dazzleman fans . . . if we get caught."

There was an uncomfortable silence. They had all thought about the possibility of getting caught, and none of them liked the idea.

"Have to think of these things," Marcus continued. "I mean, Dazzleman's got so many fans, there must have been other times when someone's tried to break into the house just to get a glimpse of him. Yes, that's a good idea. If any of us does get caught, we just say that's why we tried to get into the house—to see our hero."

"Huh." Kimberley was scornful. "Any real Dazzleman fan would know that he's disappeared. They wouldn't go looking for him at his house right now."

"Ah, but he may be—"

Furious looks from the other two stopped Stewie just in time. Kimberley didn't know the full extent of their suspicions. She thought they were just breaking into the house to find clues to Dazzleman's whereabouts, not because they hoped to find the superstar himself. And, knowing Kimberley's taste for talking, the less she knew the better.

121

They were interrupted by the sound of a motor vehicle drawing up outside the yard. Kimberley leaned forward to look through a crack in the shed wall, and they heard the engine reversing and the crunch of wheels on paving as the van backed into the yard, only a few yards away from them.

There was a long silence. Then a triumphant whisper from Kimberley. "We're in luck. It *is* Tony Spink."

They took turns to look out of the spyhole. They saw Mrs. Dolan appear at the back door of the restaurant and greet Tony Spink. She seemed pleased to see him. He lifted up the sliding metal back of the van and reached inside for a plastic tray of fish. He took this into the storage-room and returned to the van with the empty tray. He repeated the process three more times. When all four trays were back inside the van, he pulled down the metal door. He hooked the tag at the bottom of it over a metal hoop, but did not lock it. Then, whistling cheerily, he went in through the back door of the restaurant.

Marcus looked at his watch as they all waited in silence. After exactly two minutes, he said, "Right, let's go!"

The shed door opened, and the four of them came out into the yard, with Marcus leading. He unhooked the tag of the door and rolled it gently up. Through the space at the bottom the other three climbed into the van. Puffing slightly, Marcus followed. They pulled the door down till all the light was shut out.

The whole operation had taken less than thirty seconds.

"It's very dark," Kimberley whimpered.

"Just keep still for a few minutes and your eyes will get used to it."

Marcus was right. Through small chinks in the van's walls, a little light filtered, and soon they could make out the outlines of the interior. Along one side was a series of cupboards with heavy metal doors.

"That's for the frozen stuff," murmured Marcus. "We're lucky the whole van isn't refrigerated. Otherwise we might arrive at Pegler's Hall as four snowmen."

Kimberley shivered. "It's cold enough, anyway."

The rest of the space was littered with white plastic trays and boxes. Up in the front, just behind the driver's cab, was a pile of boxes, over which two old gray blankets were draped. "That's where we go," said Marcus.

They removed the blankets and made space for themselves among the boxes. It wasn't very comfortable, but it would have to do.

Then they managed to pull the blankets back up over the pile.

"Do you think he'll be able to see us if he opens the back again?" Kimberley squeaked.

"Not unless he looks closely," Marcus replied. "Let's just pray that he doesn't."

They lay there in silence for a few minutes. Then Kimberley let out another little squeak.

"Oh, do shut up, Kim!"

"I heard something."

"Don't be silly."

"I did. I really did. I heard something move." Her voice changed to a little wail. "There's someone else in the van with us!"

"No, there isn't!"

"There is. Really! Listen."

They were silent. And all seemed silent in the back of the van.

Then Kimberley squealed again. "There it was!"

"There wasn't anything."

"There was!"

"Ssh! Let's listen again."

They did. The silence grew longer. Then Emma thought she did hear something. A little movement, a little scraping noise from the back of the van. She held her breath.

It came again. A definite, scraping, scuttling noise.

"There *is* something," Marcus hissed.

"Oh, no!" Kimberley quavered. "It'll come and get us!"

"It won't. Sssh!"

They all strained their ears again. This time there was no doubt. Something was moving, scraping, rubbing against one of the boxes at the back of the van.

Suddenly there was a new noise. A strange, spluttering noise, like air coming out of the neck of a balloon. It seemed to be coming from right in the middle of them.

124

Emma was the first to realize that the new noise was Stewie laughing. "Stewie! What on earth's the matter?"

It took him some time to get the words out through his giggles. "I've just realized what it is. The other noise."

"What?"

"It's . . . the lobsters. Dazzleman's lobsters. There must be two of them in a box at the back."

Marcus started giggling, too. "Of course. How stupid of us. Yes, that's what it must be."

"But do you mean," asked Kimberley, "that they're *alive*?"

"Oh, yes. If you want fresh lobster, you buy them while they're alive. They're still alive when they get plunged into boiling water. That's how you cook lobsters."

"*Ugh!*" said Kimberley.

They suddenly felt the van jolt, and were all silent.

They heard the engine start. Tony Spink, in his cab, must have been only inches away from them. At least thank goodness he hadn't checked what was in the back before he got in.

They lurched forward as the van moved. They felt it slowly turn out of the yard into the street. They felt it build up speed till they were bouncing in the back like peas on a drum.

"Right," whispered Marcus. "Pegler's Hall—here we come!"

The journey, which can't have been more than three miles, seemed to take forever. Their position among the boxes and under the smelly blankets was far from comfortable, but not sure when they would arrive at their destination, they did not dare to relax. They stayed where they were and put up with the jolting and rattling.

At last, after one or two false alarms, the van slowed down and came to a standstill. They heard Tony Spink get out of his cab, then after about a minute they heard him return. He kept the engine running all the time.

"Ringing the bell at the gates," Marcus suggested.

This was confirmed when they heard the scrape of metal on stone as the gates were opened, and then the crunch of gravel under the van's tires as it moved forward.

They had broken through the outer defenses. They were going up the drive to Pegler's Hall.

"Now when we move," Marcus hissed, "we've got to move *fast!*"

The van crunched to a halt. They heard the engine switched off, then the driver's door opened and shut. Slowly footsteps on the gravel moved around the van to the back.

The rattle of the metal door being raised sounded monstrously loud.

The Three Detectives and Kimberley held their breath.

It seemed to take a long time. They heard the scrape of a cardboard box on the metal floor of the van. Then they heard Tony's voice, cheerily asking, "Shall I put them in the utility room, as usual?"

126

"No. Straight in the kitchen. I'll show you."

It was Stick's deep, mournful voice. The three in the van thought about his past and shuddered.

But there was no time to change their minds now. They had to move fast.

"Now!" said Marcus.

They threw off the blankets and moved to the back of the van. Their limbs were stiff and achy after being so long in the same position, but they didn't have time to worry about that.

Tony Spink had left the door at the back of the van up about two feet. Stewie got there first and poked out his tousled head to see if the coast was clear.

"No one in sight. Quick! Follow me!"

He slid down off the back of the van, and the other three did the same. Marcus, who felt his extra weight when there was rushing around to be done, came last.

It was after six o'clock and beginning to get dark, but they still blinked at the sudden daylight after the gloom beneath their blankets.

They were around the back of Pegler's Hall. The mansion's back door was open, but Stewie restrained himself from rushing straight in. That must have been the way to the kitchen where Tony Spink and Stick had just gone. It would be a terrible waste for the Three Detectives to rush straight into the arms of their enemy.

About twenty yards from the back door was a thick hedge, which surrounded a large green tank for heating

127

oil. That would hide them. Stewie made for it, and the others followed.

From behind the tank, through the branches of the hedge, they had a good view of the back door. Only a few seconds after they had hidden, Tony Spink emerged. The tall figure of Stick was close behind, as if afraid to let the deliveryman out of his sight.

"Same order tomorrow?" asked Tony.

"Till further notice," Stick grunted.

"I can't help wondering," said Tony, "with Dazzleman being away, who's getting through all these lobsters."

"You're not paid to wonder," Stick snapped. "Start wondering and you're going to lose a very nice regular order. You aren't the only fishmonger in the world."

"O.K., O.K." Tony Spink raised a hand to show he wasn't going to argue and got into the van. "I'll stop wondering," he said, as he started the engine.

"I'll come down and open the gate for you," said Stick.

"Tight security you have here," the deliveryman observed through his window.

"Yes. There are video-cameras on every entrance. No one gets in unless I know about it."

Unaware of how untrue his words were, the tall roadie started to walk down the gravel drive toward the front gates. The delivery van slowly drove along behind him.

When they were about thirty yards away, Marcus gave a signal. The Three Detectives and Kimberley scampered from behind the oil tank and in through the back door.

They were inside Pegler's Hall.

## ☆ ☆ ☆ 16 ☆ ☆ ☆

# Inside Pegler's Hall

The Three Detectives and Kimberley hurried along a passage and found themselves in a huge kitchen, which seemed to contain every labor-saving machine that had ever been invented. On the large wooden table in the middle stood a cardboard box. Thin gray reed-like things pointed out of the top and twitched. There was a scraping noise.

"Dazzleman's lobsters," said Stewie, pleased to have been proved right.

But Marcus knew there was no time for chatting. "We've got to be quick and we've got to be organized. Two of us will search the whole house, see if there's any sign of Dazzleman. Emma and Stewie, you do that. Make sure you open every door and cupboard. If any are locked, knock and see if there's anyone inside."

"What about us?" asked Kimberley.

"We'll keep lookout. I'll go on the back door, you go on the front. Make sure it's unlocked, so that we can get out quickly if we have to."

"Oow," Kimberley complained. "I wanted to see all Dazzleman's things. I wanted to—"

"Do as you're told!" Marcus bellowed. "Go on, you two! We've got about three minutes before Stick'll be back from the gate."

Emma and Stewie rushed off, with Kimberley following more slowly. They found the hall and quickly agreed that Emma should do upstairs while Stewie did the ground floor. Kimberley went to the front door and unlocked it. She peered through a glass panel in the door just in time to see the fishmonger's van passing through the gates into the gathering gloom. She watched the tall figure of Stick as, in an unhurried manner, he closed the gates and locked them.

To her relief, he did not come straight back to the house. Instead he appeared to be inspecting something on one of the trees near the gate. Kimberley did not know what it was, but one of the Three Detectives would have recognized that he was checking the video-cameras.

When he was satisfied with these, Stick set off walking around the inside of the garden's walls. Kimberley didn't know what he was doing, though one of the Three Detectives might have guessed that he was checking the other security devices, having a final look around the property before night set in.

Whatever Stick was doing, it was good news for the four in the house. The longer he took coming back, the longer they had for their search.

Kimberley relaxed a little and started to look around.

She realized that she was actually *in* one of her dreams. To be inside Dazzleman's home was just about the most exciting thing she could imagine. The only thing more exciting in the world would be to be with Dazzleman himself.

The hall was huge and beautifully furnished. Kimberley looked around in delight. And over on the far wall she could see . . . Were they? Was it possible? Her heart fluttered with excitement.

Yes, the framed circles of gleaming metal couldn't be anything else. Some shiny gold, some silvery to look at. They were the Gold and Platinum Discs that Reddimixx had won for the huge sales of their records.

Kimberley went across the hall to have a closer look.

The upstairs of Pegler's Hall seemed to stretch for miles. Bedroom after bedroom was revealed as Emma opened door after door. And there seemed to be as many bathrooms and lavatories as there were bedrooms. There were game-rooms too, and sitting-rooms and studies.

All were extravagantly furnished. Given more time, Emma would have liked to look at the flamboyant decorations in more detail. As it was, she could only note the one fact that all the rooms had in common. There was nobody in any of them.

Finally, she came upon another little staircase that she thought must lead up to some attic rooms.

She hesitated. It would be terrible to get trapped up there by the returning Stick. Still, there had been no warning sound from downstairs. And they had to make the search as thorough as possible.

Emma hurried up the little staircase.

Stewie was having the same success downstairs. The number of the rooms amazed him. So did their magnificence and the range of their decorations. Some were like ancient castles, some like space-age fantasies. One, unexpectedly, contained a heated swimming pool, surrounded by palm trees. In another there were two huge snooker tables.

He had one ugly moment. He walked into a small room near the front door and was shocked to see Stick's face staring straight at him.

It took a second before he realized that he was seeing the face on a television screen. The little room contained two banks of television monitors, and the pictures relayed were those from the video-cameras at the mansion's entrances.

Stick had been looking straight into the one by the back gate, checking that the lens was not obstructed.

So, after the moment of shock, Stewie felt encouraged. At least he knew where the enemy was, and knew he had a little longer to finish his search.

He checked out the remaining rooms on the ground floor. But all of them, like those Emma found upstairs, were empty.

Marcus couldn't see the main gates from his vantage-point by the back door, but he could see a long stretch of the outer wall of the garden. With satisfaction he noted, through the quickly thickening dusk, the tall figure of Stick making his tour of inspection. If he went all the way around, Marcus calculated, it would be a good twenty minutes before the roadie came back to the house. Which was plenty of time for a thorough search.

If Dazzleman was inside Pegler's Hall, the other two detectives would certainly find him in that time.

Even when Stick went out of vision around a corner of the building, Marcus still felt secure. After all, in only a few moments, the tall figure would be visible from the front door.

And Kimberley was safely stationed as lookout on the front door.

Kimberley couldn't believe it was happening to her. She walked along the hall, stepping over the rugs that lay on its polished wooden floor, and looked at the display of Dazzleman's triumphs.

On the wall were all the Gold Discs, from *Love Gone Missing* onward. The Platinum Discs were there, too. And lots of awards. Awards from Britain, from America, from all over the world. There were *Daily Mirror* Rock and Pop Awards for Best Single. For Best Group. Best Male Vocalist.

Kimberley Dolan was in heaven. Her mind was miles away, as she dreamed of all the things she would tell her friends.

Her mind was so far away that it was a terrible shock

to hear close behind her a harsh male voice demand, "And what are you up to, young lady?"

She whirled around, and saw, advancing toward her, a man with one ear.

All Three Detectives heard Kimberley's scream at the same moment, and all immediately rushed toward the hall.

Stewie, who had been nearest when she screamed, got there first. He stopped in the doorway of the hall and took in the scene before him.

Kimberley cowered against the wall of awards. Between her and Stewie stood the man with one ear. He had his back to the boy and was slowly moving toward the frightened girl.

Stewie thought fast and moved faster.

On tiptoe he sped across the polished floor. He was just behind as the one-eared man stepped onto one of the loose rugs.

Stewie dropped to his knees and, grabbing hold of the back of the rug, snatched it upward with all his strength.

The surprise of the attack was enough. The rug slid on the smooth surface, and the one-eared man, caught off balance, pitched forward. Kimberley dodged sideways as his head smashed against the wall. The framed Platinum Disc for *Hearts Won't Be the Only Thing (That'll Get Broken)*, dislodged by the impact, fell down and caught him on the back of his neck.

At the same moment Emma came scuttering down the main staircase, and a panting Marcus appeared from the back of the house.

"Front door," he wheezed.

Emma reached out her hand to the trembling Kimberley, and with her in tow, the Three Detectives rushed out onto the gravel drive of Pegler's Hall.

It was now nearly dark.

"Come on!" yelled Stewie. "The front gates! We can climb over!"

He burst into a sprint, but slowed when he realized the others couldn't keep up with him. Marcus was not built for running, and Emma was hampered by the terrified Kimberley.

They were about thirty yards from the gates and thought they were safe, when a tall figure jumped out of the dark bushes in front of them.

"Stop right there!" boomed Stick's deep voice.

Grabbing Marcus and Emma by the hand, Stewie suddenly changed direction and leaped sideways into the bushes. They scampered on a little through the undergrowth, then, realizing that the noise was giving away their position, froze in silence.

They could hear, horribly close, the crunch of Stick's shoes on the gravel, but he did not seem for the moment to want to go into the bushes after them.

They soon found out the reason why.

"Al!" they heard him shout up toward the house. "Al!

135

There's some kids in the garden! Put the outside lights on! And bring a flashlight! We'll get them!"

The Three Detectives and Kimberley waited, not breathing. They all prayed that Al (which must have been the name of the one-eared man) had been knocked out by his fall and would not be able to join in the chase.

But their luck was out. Suddenly the whole Elizabethan splendor of Pegler's Hall blazed into life as spotlights were switched on.

Near the house it was now as light as day, but they were still too far away, too deeply in the bushes to be seen.

Then, more threatening, another light moved from the front door of the mansion and started to come down the drive toward them.

It was the powerful beam of a flashlight, and it flickered to and fro as the one-eared man walked.

They were still all holding hands, and each could feel the other's grasp tighten. Still they froze. Still they tried not to breathe.

"Did you see them?" asked Stick's voice, as Al approached.

"Saw one. Girl," came the gruff reply. "Then one of them tripped me. Smashed my head into the wall. Just wait till I get my hands on them! I'll make them sorry they was ever born."

Stewie heard the beginnings of a sound from Kimberley, and clamped his hand over her mouth before the cry could be heard.

"They went in this side," said Stick's voice. The beam of the flashlight raked through the bushes. "Let's keep together, Al, and slowly work up the drive. I want to get all four of them. They must have been making for the gates. Let's go down that way first. Keep your eyes skinned, in case any of them try to make a break for it."

The voice and the footsteps on gravel got quieter as the two men moved down the drive. "Lie on the ground," Marcus hissed. "It's our only hope. And, Kimberley, lie on your tummy. If the flashlight catches on that glitter of yours, we're finished."

Slowly and silently, the four lowered their bodies down to the ground. "Arms over your faces," murmured Marcus, "and pull your jumpers up over your hands. Skin really shows up in the light."

They heard the voices and footsteps draw nearer. They saw the tongues of light licking through the bushes, closer and ever closer. Their bodies were rigid with fear.

Then the men were right next to them, and the light pointing right at them. Still they did not move.

Neither the light nor the footsteps moved either, for a long, long moment.

Finally, with mutters of annoyance, the two men moved their search on, up toward the house.

Marcus let them get a good twenty yards away before he tapped the others gently. "Slowly through the bushes," he breathed. "Keep under cover as long as possible. Then dash for the gate!"

They did as he said, still hand in hand, edging toward

the gate and the freedom of the road beyond. Stewie led, followed by Marcus, then Emma and Kimberley.

They had covered about half the distance, when Emma felt a little tug at her hand. Kimberley had stopped and was looking back toward Pegler's Hall.

"What's the matter?" Emma hissed.

"I just wanted one more look at *his* house."

"Kimberley, for heaven's sake!"

The men had heard something. The beam of the flashlight swung back down the drive. Kimberley was facing it when the light came, and her Dazzleman sweatshirt beamed its message back.

"Down there!" Stick's voice shouted, and the heavy footsteps of the two men pounded down the gravel.

"Run!" yelled Stewie, and sprinted out onto the drive toward the gate.

He reached it first and waited, his hands forming a stirrup for Emma. She put her foot in it and launched herself up onto the crisscross railings of the gate.

Stewie sprang up after her from a standing jump.

Emma made it to the top, flipped herself over, and dropped to safety on the other side.

Stewie could have done the same, but again he waited, one arm hooked on the railings, while the other reached down toward the puffing figure of Marcus. The two men were getting closer and closer.

Marcus's hands found Stewie's, and the younger boy yanked the heavy body up. Marcus grabbed at the railings just as Stick's hand closed on his foot.

138

Marcus kicked free, losing his shoe in the process, and reached up to the top of the gate. Stewie, who was already there, vaulted neatly over and dropped on the other side.

Marcus, with a superhuman effort, hauled himself to the top. For a moment his body balanced there, as if unsure which way it was going to fall. Then, finally, it toppled to safety.

The Three Detectives picked themselves up and belted along the wall toward the center of Pegler's End. Every second they feared the sound of the gates opening and the thud of pursuing footsteps.

But they heard nothing. Stick and Al had decided not to bother. They had let them get away.

The Three Detectives slowed to a halt. Emma and Stewie leaned against the wall, gulping for air. Marcus sat on the ground, his body flopped forward, gasping.

Emma was the first to come to her senses.

"Oh, no!" she said. "Where's Kimberley?"

# ☆ ☆ ☆ 17 ☆ ☆ ☆

# Blackthorn Cottage

Stewie looked grim. "They must have caught her."

Marcus was still too out of breath to speak.

Emma punched a fist into her hand with annoyance. "We should never have taken her. She's not one of the Three Detectives, and we shouldn't have let her come. If there'd just been the three of us, we wouldn't be in this mess now."

"If there'd just been the three of us," Stewie reminded her gently, "we wouldn't have got into Pegler's Hall in the first place. We needed Kim's help to find out about the delivery of the lobsters."

Emma had to admit that this was true.

"But," gasped Marcus, who was still sitting down, "was getting into Pegler's Hall worth doing anyway? We went in to try to find Dazzleman. And did we?"

Stewie shook his head. "He wasn't downstairs."

"Wasn't upstairs either," said Emma.

"Are you sure you both looked everywhere?"

"Yes, I went through every room upstairs. Even the attics. There was no one there. I was just double-checking when I heard Kimberley scream."

"Same with me. He certainly wasn't downstairs."

"Hmm." Slowly Marcus rose to his feet. He looked down ruefully at his one shoeless foot, but didn't comment on it. "I wonder if there was some secret place that we missed."

"Why do you say that?"

"Well, partly it's because we reckoned Dazzleman was definitely there and we didn't find him . . ."

"And what's the other reason?"

"The other reason is the second man. The one Stick called Al."

"What about him?"

"He seemed to appear very suddenly. I mean, I'm sure Kimberley screamed as soon as she saw him, and we got there only seconds later, and there he was right in the middle of the room."

"And you're wondering if he appeared from some secret hiding-place inside the house?"

"That's exactly what I'm wondering. I know he didn't come past me through the back door. And he couldn't have come in through the front door without Kimberley seeing him. You'd think she'd have screamed then—not waited until he was right in the room with her. Assuming, of course, that she was keeping lookout like she was supposed to."

Emma sighed. "I don't know whether we *can* assume

141

that in Kim's case. It wouldn't surprise me if she was just looking 'round Dazzleman's house, you know, because she was so excited to be there. I mean, if she hadn't turned 'round for 'one more look at his house,' she wouldn't have got caught and she'd be with us now. No, I think she started looking 'round, forgot about the door, and our one-eared friend just walked in and surprised her."

Marcus nodded glumly. "You're probably right. Just a minute, though—did you say 'our one-eared friend'?"

"Yes, I did. I doubt if you got the time to look at him, but he did have only one ear. Al was definitely the bloke who drove the car when Dazzleman disappeared."

"That would make sense, wouldn't it?" said Stewie. "If Al's working with Stick and if Stick really did make Dazzleman walk out of the studio at gunpoint . . ."

"Oh, yes, it all falls into place," Marcus agreed. "The only thing we're missing is the answer to the question we started out with—where is Dazzleman?"

"Well, unless we believe in your theory of a secret hiding-place," said Stewie, "he isn't in Pegler's Hall."

"No. But Kimberley is." Emma looked at her watch. Amazingly, after everything that had happened, it was still only half-past six. "In a couple of hours Kim's Mum is going to start worrying about where she is. She'll ring my Mum and ask if Kim's still with me. Then they'll both be even more worried. We must somehow get Kim out of there."

"How do you suggest doing it?" asked Marcus. "I

can't think that they'll be expecting more deliveries of lobsters tonight. And, even if they were, I think Stick might check the contents of the van a bit more carefully this time."

"Yes. There must be another way of getting in."

"Past all those video-cameras?" Marcus shook his head. "I don't see how. If only we had someone with a bit of inside knowledge of the layout of Pegler's Hall . . ."

"Layout, yes," Emma murmured. She didn't sound as if she was concentrating. Her mind was elsewhere, thinking back, trying to remember something that might suddenly become important. She turned to Stewie. "The studio was downstairs, I suppose, was it?"

"Studio?" He looked blank. "What studio?"

"There is a recording studio in Pegler's Hall. Bill the chauffeur told me. That's where they made the latest single. I went through every room upstairs, and it certainly wasn't there."

"Well, it wasn't downstairs either. I'm absolutely certain about that," said Stewie.

Emma gave a little jump and clapped her hands. "Do you realize what this means? There *is* somewhere we missed out in our search—a secret hiding-place in Pegler's Hall. And I'll bet that's where Dazzleman's been hidden. In the studio."

"But just a minute," Marcus argued. "Even if we could get back into the house—which, let's face it, is pretty unlikely—how are we going to find the place? You

143

and Stewie didn't see any sign of it last time. And if you—"

Emma was in no mood to be slowed down by reason. "We are going to find it," she announced, "by asking someone where it is. Someone who knows the house inside out. Someone who may have ideas of how we can make another break-in. And someone who—very conveniently—happens to live right here in Pegler's End."

"Bill the chauffeur!"

"Exactly, Stewie," said Emma.

Blackthorn Cottage was like its owner, low and thick-set.

But the lights inside looked warm and comforting, and once he had gotten over the surprise of the Three Detectives' arrival, Bill welcomed them warmly. He ushered them into his small living-room, where a log fire blazed.

With help from the boys, Emma gave him a quick summary of everything that had happened that evening. She also told Bill of the connection of his former employer, Dazzleman, with a group called Johnny Fann and the Fannfares.

When he heard about Stick's past, and the fact that Stick used to be called Terry Walton, Bill banged his hand on the table.

"That would explain it! That explains so much!"

"Like what?" asked Stewie.

"Like the way Stick suddenly had a job with Dazzleman. The group's been around three years, and in that time it's built up a good team of roadies. Most of

144

them have been with Reddimixx from the start, and they're a loyal bunch. So it was a bit of a surprise when Dave suddenly introduced this bloke we'd never seen before and said he was going to be a roadie for the band."

"When was that?"

"About six months ago. In fact, it was just 'round the time that Dave started to get exceptionally jumpy and nervous. I'd put that down to the fact that the latest single wasn't selling quite so well, but it makes much more sense for it to have been caused by Stick's sudden reappearance. He'd obviously got some hold over Dave— otherwise he wouldn't have been given the job so easily. Over the last six months, Stick's been getting more powerful. He's been taking responsibility for more and more areas of the group's life—and particularly of Dazzleman's life."

"If he had that sort of hold over Dazzleman," suggested Marcus, "he could easily have made his master write all those letters—the one that gave you the Big E and so on."

"You're right. That would explain it."

Stewie looked thoughtful. "But what could it be that would give someone a hold like that over another person?"

"They must both know about some dark secret," said Bill, "something that happened a long time ago and that Dazzleman wants to be kept quiet."

"He wants his real age kept quiet," said Marcus.

Bill gave a little snort of laughter. "That's true. He's

145

not keen on the whole world knowing he's forty, I agree. But it must be something more serious than that."

"I wonder if it's anything to do with the murder?" said Emma softly.

"Murder?"

Quickly she filled Bill in on the events that had taken place twenty years before in a car-park in Salford. At the end of her narration, he whistled. "This is more serious than I thought. Stick never seemed that sort to me. Always seemed a nice enough bloke. Quiet, self-contained, but nice enough." He let out another low whistle. "And to think that he's a murderer."

"That's the main reason why we are worried about Kimberley." Marcus brought the subject back to the present day with considerable urgency.

"And why we've got to get back inside Pegler's Hall to rescue her—" added Stewie.

"And rescue Dazzleman." Emma completed the sentence.

"But I thought you said you'd been right through the place and hadn't seen no sign of him," Bill objected. "Surely you can't still think he's in there?"

"Oh, but we do," said Emma. "We think he's in the one place we didn't look because we couldn't find it, and that's in—"

Bill nodded as she spoke and they said the words together: "—the studio."

"You mean there really is one?" Stewie bounced with excitement.

"Oh, yes. There most certainly is. Very splendid studio—got all the latest recording equipment, the lot. And now I come to think of it, it would make a very good prison. Soundproof, for a start. Also, it's extremely well-hidden."

"Where?"

"Well, you know Pegler's Hall is a really old house . . ."

"Elizabethan, the original parts of it."

"That's right, Marcus. Well, I'm not too hot on English history, but I gather there was a time when there was big religious arguments between Protestants and Roman Catholics—and you got into trouble if you was a Roman Catholic."

"In the seventeenth century. 'Round the time of the Civil War," said Marcus.

"Anyway, 'round that time, whenever it was, a lot of the big Catholic families still liked to have their own priest conduct their church services for them—even though it was against the law. And, in case people came 'round who might report them if they saw this priest bloke, the family hid him. They had a secret place built specially."

"A priest's hole."

"That, Marcus my son, is the very expression. Well, it seems that Pegler's Hall used to be owned by a Catholic family . . ."

"And it's got its own priest's hole?"

"It certainly has. Mind you, I don't think the priest it

was made for would recognize it now—unless he was used to laying his sermons down on twenty-four-track recording machines."

"You mean the priest's hole is the studio?"

"Spot on. The space has been enlarged, dug out till it's a big room right under the house. But the way in hasn't been touched—it's still the secret entrance to the priest's hole."

"Where is the secret entrance?"

"Which one of you searched the ground floor?"

"I did," said Stewie.

"Well, do you remember the dining-room? Great big place with stained-glass windows . . ."

"I remember it."

"You may have noticed it's got a dirty great carved stone fireplace."

"Yes, I saw that."

"There's carvings of roses down each side of that fireplace. All the roses look the same, but one's different. Third one down on the left-hand side. That is like the key to the priest's hole. If you turn that 'round clockwise, you'll hear a click, and then a whole panel in the wall beside the fireplace will open. That is the way to the studio."

"Brilliant!" Stewie leaped into the air. "That's where Dazzleman must be! Come on, let's get back into Pegler's Hall and rescue him!"

"Just a minute," said Marcus with his usual infuriating calm. "There's something you're forgetting. We don't know how to get back into Pegler's Hall."

"Oh, that's true." Stewie looked as deflated as a balloon that has just met a pin.

"That was the other thing we wanted to ask you about," said Emma to Bill. "You know that place inside out. Have you any idea of how we could make a second break-in?"

The chauffeur's face looked glum.

"I mean, we know you had to give back your keys, but we thought you might have some other ideas."

"Keys is no problem." As he spoke, the chauffeur reached into a drawer and threw down a large bunch on the table. "I was always afraid of losing them, so I had a set of duplicates made."

"Brilliant! So we can just walk in!" Stewie's balloon of excitement had blown itself up again.

But Bill was shaking his head. "It's not actually getting through the doors that's difficult, it's getting through the doors *unseen*. No doubt you've noticed the video-cameras on the main gates?"

The Three Detectives nodded, quieter now.

"Well, there's a similar set-up on every other possible entrance."

"What about climbing over the wall?" asked Stewie.

But the shake of Bill's head showed that it wouldn't work, either. "The wall, all the way 'round, is wired up to an alarm system. Any intruder touches the top of that, and a siren sounds right through the grounds."

"We're not very heavy," said Stewie hopefully. "Maybe we wouldn't set it off."

"No such luck, I'm afraid. Very sensitive system. I

can't think how many times I've been called out by the siren only to discover that it was set off by a cat on the wall."

"Oh, dear." Gloom descended on the Three Detectives.

"It's so frustrating!" Emma complained. "To know where the secret hiding place is, to have keys to the building—and then not to be able to get inside!"

"I'm afraid that's the way it is," said Bill. "And after tonight's excitements, Stick and his mate are going to be watching those monitors from the video-cameras like hawks." He sighed. "No, I'm afraid there's no chance." Then he added, in a voice that made the situation sound hopeless, "Unless, of course, one of you can think of a way of putting those video-cameras out of action."

An enormous grin spread across Stewie's freckled face.

"I can," he said.

# ☆ ☆ ☆ 18 ☆ ☆ ☆

# The Priest's Hole

Bill did exactly as they asked him. First he drove the mile back to Stewie's house, then waited in the car with Marcus while the other two went in. Stewie disappeared into the back garden, while Emma asked Mrs. Hinde politely if she might use the telephone.

First she rang Mrs. Dolan. She said she was sorry that Kimberley was late, but she should be home within the hour. Then she rang her stepmother to apologize for being late herself and to say that she too would be home within the hour. In both cases she put the phone down before either mother had time to argue.

Marcus didn't bother to ring his home. His parents were off on another foreign trip, and Kirsten was used to him keeping his own hours.

As Stewie hurried through the house with a large bundle under his arm, his mother asked if he was really going out again. He said yes, snatched up a pair of one of his brothers' running shoes, and, grabbing Emma by

the hand, whisked her out of the front door before his
mother had time to say anything else.

He gave the shoes to Marcus, who put them on. Then
Stewie loaded his bundle into Bill's Mini, and they all set
off back to Pegler's Hall.

The chauffeur parked a good hundred yards away from
the main gates, well out of range of the prying cameras.
The group stayed in the car while Marcus ran through
the plan for the last time.

"We won't have long, but I think it'll be long enough.
When Stewie's done his stuff, we open the main gate
with Bill's key and rush inside, making sure to lock it
after us. We go straight into the bushes where we hid last
time. I think we can count on Stick and Al coming down
to the main gate. While they're doing that, we move
quickly but quietly up to the house. If it's locked, we use
Bill's key; if it's unlocked we just go straight in. Stewie,
you know your way around the ground floor, so you
must lead us straight to the dining-room. Once we're in
there, we open the priest's hole, get down to the studio,
and free Dazzleman."

"And free Kimberley, too," said Stewie. "I bet they'll
have locked her up in the same place."

Emma giggled. "That would be her idea of heaven—
to be locked up in the same room as Dazzleman. On the
other hand, she might have wished for it to happen under rather different circumstances."

"Are you sure I shouldn't be coming with you?" Bill's

voice sounded worried. "I don't like the idea of you kids being in there on your own. I mean, if there's any rough stuff—"

"If it's just us," said Emma, "there's much less likely to be any rough stuff. If we do get caught, we can pretend that we are just more daft Dazzleman fans, who'd do anything to get inside their idol's house."

"But suppose Kimberley's talked," Bill objected. "Suppose she's told them the real reason why you're breaking in."

"She doesn't know enough for that to be a problem," Emma replied. "She knows we're looking for Dazzleman, and she knows we think he's been kidnapped, but she doesn't know anything about Stick's involvement—and she certainly doesn't know anything about Stick's past."

"Hmm." Bill still didn't sound happy. "I just don't want any of you to get hurt. I really think we ought to bring in the police."

"No, Bill," said Emma firmly. "Not yet. We'll do as we agreed. You wait out here for exactly half an hour after we've gone through the gate. If we're not out by then, call the police by all means."

"All right," said Bill grudgingly.

The Three Detectives got out of the Mini. Stewie opened the trunk and took out his bundle. He removed the sheet to reveal—the Stewart Hinde Mark Three Gunge-Spludger!

He stroked the cylinder of the barrel lovingly. "I knew we'd find a use for you, old thing," he said.

"Aren't you going to put it on the stand?" asked Emma.

"I'm not sure yet. It depends on where I fire it from. If I do it from ground-level, the cameras may catch me setting the thing up, and then the whole idea falls apart."

"But where else can you do it from?" asked Marcus. They were walking along carefully toward the main gate of Pegler's Hall.

"I was wondering about that tree." Stewie pointed to the other side of the road just opposite the gates. "I think the cameras are pointed too far down to see anyone up there."

Emma looked doubtful. "It's a lot farther than that apple tree was from your garden shed. Do you think the Gunge-Spludger will work at that range?"

Stewie shrugged. "I hope so."

"So do I," said Marcus. "Because we aren't going to get a second chance. We need a direct hit on each camera first go, or we'll just alert Stick and his mate that there's something funny going on."

"Can the Gunge-Spludger do two shots in a row?" asked Emma anxiously. "Or will it have to be reloaded?"

"It can do two." Stewie did not sound worried. He had spent a long time getting his invention just right, and he felt confident that it would work.

He stopped on the pavement and opened his plastic ice-cream box. Using his trowel, he shovelled a lot of the gray, gooey mess into the funnel of the Gunge-Spludger.

"What on earth is that muck?" asked Marcus.

"My own recipe. It contains putty and floor-tile adhesive and oil and a few other secret ingredients."

"And you're sure it'll stick?"

"Positive. If I get a direct hit over the lens, it'll stay there till it's scraped off with a knife."

The weapon was now loaded to its inventor's satisfaction. "Right, I'll cross the road here, so that I'm out of range of the cameras. Marcus, you come across and give me a leg up into the tree. Emma, you stay on this side. Now, when I get up there I'm going to have to find my range on the two cameras. You'll be able to hear each time I fire, but you won't be able to see whether I've made a hit or not. So don't go forward to the gates until I wave—O.K.?"

"O.K.," said the other two detectives. Stewie was in charge of this part of the operation, and they were happy to obey him.

The two boys kept close to the hedges on the other side of the road until they were behind the tree. Marcus formed a step with his hands, and Stewie heaved himself easily into the branches.

"O.K., pass up the Gunge-Spludger," he hissed down.

Marcus did as he was told. Stewie pulled the heavy cylinder up into the tree.

"Get back to the other side, Marcus. Don't cross straight over here. Go about twenty yards down the road, then there's no danger of you being seen. And remember—don't go in front of the gates until you see me wave."

155

Stewie watched his friend go and join Emma before he concentrated on setting up and aiming the Gunge-Spludger. He felt calm, and he knew he mustn't rush things. If the machine worked, it would not only help the Three Detectives in their adventure, it would also prove that he was a good inventor. He didn't want to spoil his chances by being careless.

He could see the two video-cameras quite clearly from his perch—little rectangular boxes attached on arms to trees on the far side of the gate. At the front of each, the little dull eye of the lens was pointing down at the area in front of the gates. Two all-seeing eyes, whose pictures were relayed back to the row of television monitors he had seen inside the house.

Those two eyes had to be closed.

He steadied his back against the main trunk of the tree, with his feet securely pushing against another branch. Ideally placed in front of him was the fork of two branches, and into this V he set the Gunge-Spludger. He pointed the barrel at one of the camera-lenses, then moved it around to point at the other.

That was going to be the difficult moment. Even if he was lucky and got a direct hit on the first lens, it was essential that he did the same to the second. Otherwise he would just have warned the watchers in the house of the second break-in.

He tried the movement through many times. Over on the other side of the road he could see impatience in Emma and Marcus's faces, but he did not allow himself to be hurried.

At last he was ready. He felt a little tickle of worry. The range was much farther than he had ever tried before. Suppose it wouldn't reach . . . Suppose he judged the angle wrong . . . Suppose the pile of goo just landed splat on the railings of the gate . . .

He forced such doubts from his mind and concentrated. He pulled back the handle of the Gunge-Spludger and sighted along the cylinder to the lens of the right-hand video-camera. When it was pointing directly on target, he raised the barrel till it was aiming at the tree about a foot above the lens. According to his calculations, that would be the right angle.

His whole body was steady. He took a deep breath.

Then, as he had practiced many times, he pressed the plunger smoothly into the outer cylinder.

There was a slurping sound like someone gulping a drink.

His eyes followed the shape through the air and saw it splat satisfyingly over the first lens.

Immediately, still keeping his body steady, he moved the barrel around to the second lens. As he did so, he drew back the handle and heard the comforting plop of the second lump of gunge dropping into position.

He lined up the tip of the barrel on the second lens, then raised it exactly the same distance as he had on the other side.

A second time he pressed the plunger firmly in.

A second time he watched a shapeless blob hurtle through the darkness.

157

And a second time he saw it land like a pancake over the lens.

Stewie waved to the other two detectives.

He left the Gunge-Spludger propped up in the tree and dropped to the ground. Marcus already had the key in the lock of the gate.

By the time Stewie had run across the road, the other two were inside. He slipped through after them, and Marcus locked the gates.

They plunged into the bushes out of which they had run earlier in the evening and started scrambling up toward the house.

"Freeze!" Marcus hissed.

Pegler's Hall, which had been in darkness, once again blazed with light. The front door opened and two figures emerged. One they could recognize easily by his height, and though they couldn't actually see that the other only had one ear, they knew who he was.

The Three Detectives neither moved nor breathed as the two men crunched by, within a couple of yards of them. Al once again carried the flashlight, but he was not interested in what lay in the bushes. He wanted to know what had gone wrong down by the gates.

"Now!" Marcus's order came when the men were twenty yards past them, and the Three Detectives ran on tiptoe up toward the house.

"Back door!" said Marcus. "Otherwise they'll see us."

The three rushed around to the back, out of sight of the gates. Marcus found the right key and let them in.

"Lead the way, Stewie!"

He knew exactly where to go. In less than no time they were in the dining-room. They could see the outlines of the tall stained-glass windows; the spotlights from outside splashed weird colors on the vaulted ceiling and panelled walls. A table, about thirty feet long, ran the length of the room, and at one end there was a balcony.

Stewie, who was first in, went straight to the fireplace and looked at the rose carvings.

Left-hand side. First. Second. Third one down.

He took the rose in his right hand and, breathing a prayer, turned it.

There was a click and a slight hiss as a panel beside the fireplace moved back and slid out of sight.

Light spilled out, revealing a stone staircase, leading down.

"You two go," said Emma. "I'll keep watch."

The boys nodded and disappeared down into the silence of the staircase.

Emma looked around the room. Nothing moved. She went across to the door through which they had entered. The next room was empty.

But, as she turned back, she gasped.

Slowly, but definitely, the secret panel was closing.

She rushed across the room, but it was too late. The gap had closed to nothing before she got there.

"So, we meet again!"

Once more she gasped at the sound of the voice behind her.

She looked up to the balcony.

A ghostly and horrible face glared at her. Red and green light from the stained glass windows glowed on its cheeks.

In the hand that leaned over the balcony rail was the remote control device that had closed the secret door.

It was Stick.

# ☆ ☆ ☆ 19 ☆ ☆ ☆

# Alone with a Murderer

Emma was too frightened to move, as the tall figure came slowly down the stairs from the balcony. He walked toward her. The table was still between them. On the table were rows of tall candlesticks.

Suddenly he produced a lighter from his pocket and lit three of the candles. He indicated a chair on Emma's side. "Sit."

She did as she was told, and he drew out a chair and sat down opposite. He looked into her eyes.

With bravery she did not feel, Emma returned the stare. His eyes were dark brown, and rather than being frightening, they looked full of pain.

He blinked first, and looked away. Emma felt it was a small triumph.

"What's your name?"

"Emma." She was surprised that she had any voice, but it came out sounding almost normal.

"So you decided to break in again?"

She nodded.

"Full marks for persistence, anyway." He looked over to the secret panel. "And your two friends have gone down there?"

"Yes."

"To join the other one. Kimberley."

"Yes, to join Kimberley." Boldly, Emma added, "And Dazzleman."

Stick's head jerked upward. He hadn't been expecting that.

"What makes you think Dazzleman's down there?"

"He is. We've worked it out. First, he gave me a message to say he was being kidnapped."

"How?"

"You probably don't remember, but I was in the studio the day he disappeared. So was Kimberley. My father was directing the video."

"Good grief. Yes, you do look familiar. But I didn't really notice you that day."

"You were too busy planning your kidnap to notice us. But you didn't want us there. I remember you were the only one who didn't want to give permission for us to come into the studio that day."

"And you think I was planning a kidnap?"

"Yes. But it had to look as if Dazzleman had just run off again. When he was late in the morning, you suggested that's what he might have done. You put the idea into everyone's mind."

"So how do you reckon I kidnapped him?" Stick's voice was dull and flat.

162

"You had a gun. You forced him to go out of the studio to the car-park, where your friend Al was waiting in the car. And you kept Dazzleman covered till he got into the car. What you may have forgotten, though, is that there was a girl sitting outside the studio, and Dazzleman gave her an autograph."

"I did see her. I was worried for a moment. I thought she might ruin the plan. That was you?"

"Yes."

"And the autograph he gave you was a message?"

"Yes. It was a reference to one of the songs on the second Reddimixx album. *You Can Set Me Free*. Do you know it?"

"Oh, yes," replied Stick wearily. "I know it very well."

"So that made us think Dazzleman was here—particularly the line about being a prisoner 'in my own home.' And then we found out that the order for lobsters was still being kept up, and we knew you were a vegetarian, so we knew he just had to be here."

"Full marks for detective work." Stick drummed his fingers on the table. "And if all that happened to be true . . . would you have come up with a reason why I should have done it?"

Emma took a deep breath. "It's something that happened a long time ago. I think it's a secret between you and Dazzleman. I think it goes back to the days when you were playing with Johnny Fann and the Fannfares . . . Terry."

The name of the group shocked him, but when she

said his own, all the color left his cheeks. His voice sounded strangled as he said, "You know who I am?"

"Yes. I got the whole story from Eddie Bartlett."

"Eddie? I didn't know he was still around."

"Oh, yes."

Stick's long face looked miserable. "So if he's told you the whole story, you can work out why I'm here."

"No. Not completely."

"He told you about the music, though? He told you that Dave and I used to write songs together?"

"Yes."

"Well, surely that explains it, doesn't it?"

Emma shook her head. "Not to me."

"Listen. Dave and I used to write songs. We said we did them together, but in fact we really wrote our own and then the other one would just add the odd finishing touch."

"Like John Lennon and Paul McCartney for the Beatles."

"Exactly. Well, if Eddie told you that, it should all be clear."

"But it isn't. Eddie said he could always tell from the quality of the songs which one of you had written them. He said some of the songs were brilliant and some very ordinary."

"That's right."

"And he said that Dave wrote the brilliant ones and you wrote the ordinary ones."

Stick groaned and his head flopped forward onto his arms. "Why did he say that?"

164

"He said that twenty years ago, when you were all in the group together, he never knew who was responsible for which songs. It was only when the Reddimixx singles started coming out that he knew for certain—because it said on them they were written by Dave Smith."

"Yes. 'Said on them.' But just because it said it on them, that didn't mean it was true. I wrote those songs."

"You did?"

"Yes, I wrote what you call the 'brilliant' ones, and Dave wrote the 'ordinary' ones."

"Good gracious. And is that why Reddimixx's music suddenly gets worse?"

"That is exactly why. Dave had worked through all of my old songs, and then he had to start using his own. The change in quality shows."

"But what he's done is illegal." Emma had heard from her father a little about the laws of copyright, the laws that ensure that a writer or musician is not cheated of the money owed to him for his work. "Dazzleman has no right to claim the songs if he didn't write them!"

"No, he has no right. But he reckoned he'd get away with it. You see, he was only going to be in trouble if I suddenly appeared and claimed the songs. And I was out of the country."

"Oh, yes." Emma felt a little tremor of fear. She had suddenly remembered why Stick was out of the country.

"Dave thought he was safe. Perhaps he thought I'd never find out about what he'd done. But the success of Reddimixx was so massive that there was nowhere in the world that I wasn't going to hear about it sooner or later.

I was working in Australia when I heard the first single, *Love Gone Missing*. I wrote that song in 1963. Well, at first I thought, blooming cheek, still, good luck to him, let him use one of my songs to get started, see if I care. But then, as he did more and more of them, and they were more and more successful and I couldn't pick up a newspaper without reading how much money he was making, I couldn't stand it any longer. I knew I had to come back and claim some of what was owed to me.

"So I got a false passport with a false name, and I came back to England for the first time in twenty years. As soon as he saw me, Dave knew why I had come. First thing he said was how pleased he was to see me, and how he'd been trying to find me, so that I could get my share of the record royalties. He's got a cheek, you have to hand it to him. He gave me a job as road manager and said he'd sort out a deal as soon as possible to see that I got the money that was owed to me."

"But he didn't sort out the deal?"

Stick shook his head. "No, he didn't. There was always some excuse, some legal problem, some reason it had to be held up. After a few months I realized he was never going to do it unless I made him."

"So you kidnapped him?"

"That's what I did. I chose a time when he really needed to be around—half-way through the video, final mix on the new single not decided, promotional tour being set up—and I reckoned if I locked him away long enough, he would eventually come 'round and sign a contract giving me my rights in those songs."

"You managed to get him to sign other things—the letters sacking his chauffeur and the rest of his staff."

"Oh, yes, he did those quite happily. But he's still holding out on the big one. I think it's just the money. He's got used to having so much money that he hates the idea of parting with a penny of it."

"But the money's not his! He cheated you to get it. It's not fair!" Emma was amazed to find herself so firmly on the side of her enemy.

Stick sighed. "The world, I'm afraid, Emma, is not a fair place."

"But surely," she went on, still angry, "you could have got lawyers onto him? You could have got a solicitor to sort it out for you. I mean, have you got some proof that you actually wrote the songs?"

"Oh, yes, I've got proof." Stick's dark eyes looked sadder than ever. "But lawyers . . . solicitors . . . no. I'm afraid I couldn't bring the forces of British law in to help me . . . for reasons that I can't go into."

There was a silence, then Emma said in a little voice, "I know the reasons."

"Do you?" This time there was no surprise in the face that looked into hers. It was as if he had accepted that she knew everything about him, and there was no point in arguing.

"It's because of the murder of Dusty Ellis, isn't it?"

He gave a little nod and turned his face sharply away. But he did not move it fast enough; Emma saw the pain in his dark eyes.

"That's why you had to come back under another

name. That's why you had to use the kidnap method to persuade Dazzleman that he must give you your rights. And," Emma continued, speaking as the thought came to her, "that's why Dazzleman never will sign that contract."

"What!"

"He knows he's in charge. He knows you can't keep him locked up here forever. And he knows that any moment he wants to, as soon as he's free, he can just tell the police your real name is Terry Walton, and that you're the man they've been hunting for twenty years for the murder of Dusty Ellis."

"I didn't kill him, you know."

Now it was Emma's turn to say, "What!"

"Oh, I know it looked that way, but I didn't do it. I was furiously angry with him when I went out into that car-park, and I wanted to hit him, to beat him up, but not to kill him.

"When we got outside, I don't know if Eddie told you, but a lot of the lads who'd been dancing came out after us. Some of them didn't like our music. They preferred old-fashioned rock and roll, didn't want to know about new stuff. So, though Dusty and I had gone out to fight each other, we suddenly found we were being attacked by this mob of hooligans.

"We fought them off as well as we could, but there were twenty or thirty of them, and we were losing badly.

"Then one of them drew a knife. Dusty went forward to stop him, and he stabbed Dusty in the chest.

168

"A couple more of them drew knives, and they turned on me. I ran. I ran like I've never run before in my life. And I just kept running.

"I spent the night hiding in an old, empty house, and the next morning I had only one thought—to get as far away from that place as possible. I was young then, and very frightened.

"So I went south. After a couple of days I got to Dover. From there I rang a friend who'd been at the dance and asked what'd happened. He told me. He said the police had rounded up the yobs who attacked me and Dusty, and questioned them. And, to protect themselves, the whole lot had said they'd seen me stab Dusty.

"Well, I knew it wasn't true, but I could see things looked bad for me. Dave and Eddie had seen me going out of the hall with Dusty, threatening to do all kinds of terrible things to him. And now there was a whole bunch of liars prepared to swear that they had seen me stab him in the car-park.

"I caught the next ferry out and lost myself in Europe for a few years. Then I went to Africa, then Australia.

"I've thought about it a lot since, what I should have done. By running away I made things look even worse. Perhaps if I'd given myself up to the police, I'd have been proved innocent. I don't know. All I do know, Emma, is that, like I said a few minutes ago, the world is not a very fair place."

This long narration seemed to have exhausted Stick. He slumped back in his chair. Emma looked at him with

169

pity. She knew he had been telling the truth. No one could have lied with such conviction. She tried to think of something comforting to say.

But she never got the chance to say it. At that moment a buzzer rang loudly inside the house. Stick looked up nervously. Emma glanced at her watch. Thirty-five minutes had passed since the Three Detectives had entered the gates of Pegler's Hall.

The door of the dining-room crashed open, and a harsh voice announced, "It's the police!"

Emma turned, expecting to see a uniformed policeman.

But no. Instead, the one-eared man stood in the doorway.

In his hand was a gun.

"Come on, Stick!" he urged. "It'll take them a couple of minutes to get in. We can escape the back way."

As if half-asleep, the tall sad man rose to his full height and moved across to the door.

"But what about her?" asked Al nastily. "She'll be able to tell them which way we've gone. What are we going to do about her?"

And his gun moved to point at Emma's chest.

☆ ☆ ☆ **20** ☆ ☆ ☆

# Rescue!

The silence seemed very long.

The gun remained trained on Emma.

Then she heard Stick's voice. "No. Leave her. She's done no harm."

The one-eared man looked angry, but he lowered the gun. "Come on, Stick! Let's run!"

"No," said Stick, and his voice was very weary. "You go. I'm tired of running."

Al gave his boss a look of puzzlement but didn't stay to ask questions. With the gun still in his hand, he rushed off out of sight.

Wordlessly, and as if every step were a huge effort, Stick moved across to the table and picked up the remote control device that he had left there. He pointed it at the rose on the fireplace and pressed a button.

The rose turned, and as it did so, with the same click and hiss as before, the secret door opened.

"All right," Stick shouted in a dull voice. "You can all come up now."

Then he walked to the end of the table and slumped into a throne-like chair.

Stewie and Marcus came out first. They looked frightened, and each gave a little jump as they saw the crumpled figure of Stick.

"It's all right," said Emma. "It's all all right now."

They came across to her. The Three Detectives were together again.

Kimberley came out next. Her glittery sweatshirt was crumpled, and her eyes were red with crying. More tears burst out as she rushed across to be cradled in Emma's arms.

Finally, Dazzleman emerged. But few of his fans would have recognized this creature as the silver being who flashed across stages and television screens in front of Reddimixx.

He still had on the glittery trousers he had worn on the day of his disappearance, but they were crumpled and tarnished. He had taken off the jacket, revealing a grubby-looking vest, over which very ordinary-looking suspenders held up the trousers.

He had removed the mirrors from his face, leaving little diamond shapes of pale skin. The silver make-up had mostly rubbed off, leaving his face just looking dirty. And hair, spiky hair, had grown all over his chin and shaven head.

The hair was gray.

The superstar's face was tired and puffy. He looked every one of his forty years.

But still in the brown eyes there was a light of triumph, particularly when he looked across at the figure at the end of the table.

Terry Walton did not look up at the man who had cheated him. He seemed lost in the bitterness of his own thoughts.

He just sat there quietly until the police arrived to take him away.

The Three Detectives and Kimberley were driven home in a police car.

The two boys talked excitedly all the way back. Kimberley, too, seemed to have rediscovered her unrivaled ability to chatter. Emma, though, was silent.

She spoke only once. In a moment when Kimberley paused for breath, Emma asked, "What was it like? You've always dreamed of being alone with Dazzleman, and now your dream has come true. What was he like?"

"Actually," Kimberley whispered in her ear, "he was terribly boring."

# Number One

Two weeks later at breakfast, Douglas Cobbett was in a very cheerful mood. He kissed Emma on the cheek as he entered the kitchen. "Sorry I didn't see you last night, love. Got back rather late. Still, it was worth it. We finally got the last bit of the Reddimixx film in the can."

"Was it good?"

He nodded slowly, a little smile on his lips. "Yes. Though I say it myself, it was extremely good."

"Excellent."

"And success breeds success, you know. There was a chap in the studio yesterday who manages one of the big American bands . . . what are they called—the Schmaltzes?"

"They *are* big. Their last record was Number One in the States for weeks."

"Right. Well, anyway, this guy came to watch the filming, and he liked what he saw—and he's asked me to make the Schmaltzes' next video."

"That's great. Things really seem to have turned out fine."

"Sure. Since Dazzleman's reappeared, everything's happening. Ooh, I know what I wanted to tell you . . . I had a call yesterday from the bloke who took over from me on that BBC show . . ."

"The 'Where are they now?' thing?"

"That's it. Well, you remember you thought of doing something on people who had worked with Dazzleman. . . ?"

"Yes."

"They're going ahead with it. The producer rang to thank me, so I told him it was your idea, and he asked me to pass on the thanks to you."

"You mean Eddie Bartlett's changed his mind? He's actually going to talk?"

"Yes. Not just him, either. There's another bloke they've found, who used to be with Johnny Fann and the Fannfares, and he's agreed to do the program, too. Chap called Terry Walton."

"Terry Walton? But I thought he was suspected of murder?"

Douglas Cobbett looked at his daughter with a strange expression. "You seem to know rather a lot about all this, Emma."

"Yes, I do." She did not tell her father any more than that. "What's happened about St—Terry Walton?"

"Well, I gather you know all the background, how Terry was suspected of having stabbed Dusty Ellis in a car-park in Salford back in 1965?" Emma nodded. "The police were convinced he had done it, especially when he did a bunk and went abroad. But then, a couple of years later, something happened that made them change their minds. There was a gang fight in Salford, a lot of young people got hurt with knives, and there were some arrests. While the suspects were being questioned, one of them confessed to having stabbed Dusty Ellis. So he was tried, found guilty, and sent to prison."

"And Terry Walton never knew about it?"

"No. He spent twenty years wandering the world, thinking he could never come back into this country, and all the time there was nothing against him."

"And meanwhile Dazzleman was stealing his songs."

"So you heard about that, too? But don't worry, it's all being sorted out."

"What do you mean?"

"As soon as Terry Walton found out he was a free man, he hired the best music lawyer in the country, and he's going to get back every penny that Dazzleman owes him."

"Will it be a lot?"

"On songs as successful as the Reddimixx ones, Emma, it'll run into millions of pounds."

"Excellent. And I shouldn't think Terry Walton would ever want to see Dazzleman again."

"Well, that's the strange thing about it. In spite of everything that's happened, Terry doesn't seem to bear any grudges. Not only that, he's actually quite keen to write songs for the band. It seems that he was writing all the time he was away, and he's got a great pile of material."

"So Reddimixx's music will go back to being as good as it was at first?"

"I suppose so. Oh, incidentally, talking of Reddimixx, I've got something for you."

"What?"

"You know the group's doing a big promotional tour to back the new single. Well, it starts in six weeks at the Odeon, Hammersmith. And"—Douglas Cobbett reached into his jacket as he spoke—"I've got you four tickets!" He held them up triumphantly.

At this point Tommy, who thought he had been quiet for far too long, decided that he wanted one of the Reddimixx tickets and made a lunge for them. His milk glass went flying all over his father's paper. Mrs. Cobbett shouted.

Breakfast became much as usual in the Cobbett household.

*No Love Lost* was by no means the best single Reddimixx had ever released. The first three had been much better (and the ones that followed it would be better, too, because they would be written by the same man, Terry Walton).

But when it came out, five weeks later, *No Love Lost* was an instant success. This was largely due to a very skillful video (which was later to collect the *Daily Mirror* Rock and Pop Award for the Best Video of the Year).

The record's success was also helped by the publicity for Reddimixx's forthcoming national tour. By the time that tour opened, at the Odeon, Hammersmith, *No Love Lost* was already at Number One and was destined to stay there for five weeks.

The Three Detectives and Kimberley Dolan had very good seats, and the concert was certainly a spectacular affair. The music was heard through a wall of screams. Smoke-bombs exploded, lights flooded the stage like fountains, multicolored lasers raked the auditorium. The members of the band were dressed more flamboyantly than ever, but in spite of the wildness of their costume, all eyes were on the silver figure who leaped and cavorted in the center of the stage.

Dazzleman was back! Dazzleman was a superstar!

But Emma Cobbett could not share in the Dazzleman-worship of the rest of the girls in the audience. For her the silver figure was not a superstar but a middle-aged cheat. Through the make-up she seemed to see the unshaven, puffy-faced creature who had emerged from the priest's hole in Pegler's Hall.

She looked at her companions. Kimberley Dolan was back in her simple heaven, gazing open-mouthed at the stage and screaming every time the pulse of the music demanded it. She wore a new Dazzleman catsuit. Her hair was pulled up tight into a little bun from which three tiny plaits protruded. These had been sprayed with red and green glitter. Gold varnish flashed on her fingernails.

Kimberley sighed ecstatically. "Ooh," she said, "isn't he *fantastic!*"

She seemed to have forgotten that she had ever described Dazzleman as "boring."

Emma looked at the other two.

Marcus had lost interest in the music. He had taken out a pocket video-game and was shooting dragons with electronic darts.

Stewie was gazing up at the ceiling. His mind wasn't on the music either. The distracted expression on his face meant that soon there would be another Stewart Hinde invention.

All of them had lost interest in the concert.

The Three Detectives were bored.

They needed another adventure.